Praise for Leslie Kelly

"Leslie Kelly's books are the perfect blend of sass and class. Her cheeky style makes her one of the strongest voices in romance today."
—*New York Times* bestselling author Vicki Lewis Thompson

"Leslie Kelly is a master storyteller. This book is a keeper."
—#1 *New York Times* bestselling author

"Those who enjoy Leslie Kelly's trademark humor—sexy, independent heroines and good-hearted bad boys—will not be disappointed and will certainly be back for more."
—*The Romance Reader* on *She's Got the Look*

"Ms. Kelly has a delightful and engaging voice that had me laughing out loud and relentless in reading every delicious word."
—*The Romance Readers Connection*

"Leslie Kelly continues to show why she is becoming one of Harlequin's most popular authors."
—*The Best Reviews*

"Ms. Kelly never fails to deliver a captivating story."
—*Romance Reviews Today*

"Leslie Kelly writes with a matchless combination of sexiness and sassiness that makes every story a keeper."
—*Fallen Angel Reviews*

Blaze™

Dear Reader,

After I wrote my January 2008 release, *One Wild Wedding Night,* I heard from a lot of readers who loved the concept. Wanting to go back to it, I had it in the back of my mind when writing *Play with Me—* after all, Reese had a big family, and Amanda had one sister and one very outrageous best friend.

If you read *One Wild Wedding Night,* you might remember there were five stories in all. This one's a little different. I wanted to go deeper into the lives of these characters, so I only included three complete novellas. That gave me a bit more room to explore their motivations, desires and those steamy moments.

I also put a lot of thought into the structure of this book. Each story reflects a different phase of one of my more typical stand-alone Harlequin Blaze titles. "First Kiss" is the opening—the first meet between strangers, the rise of sexual tension leading to the love scene. "Halfway There" is the middle—these two people know each other and have been dancing around what they want for a very long time. "Last Dance" (my favorite, actually) is the end....
In fact, the whole story starts at what I would consider the "black moment" in one of my novels, and sees the couple working through their differences and arriving at their happily-ever-after.

Hope you enjoyed this little glimpse into my process, and I truly hope you love the book!

Best wishes,

Leslie Kelly

Leslie Kelly

ANOTHER WILD WEDDING NIGHT

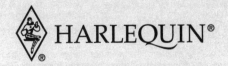

HARLEQUIN®

TORONTO • NEW YORK • LONDON
AMSTERDAM • PARIS • SYDNEY • HAMBURG
STOCKHOLM • ATHENS • TOKYO • MILAN • MADRID
PRAGUE • WARSAW • BUDAPEST • AUCKLAND

Recycling programs
for this product may
not exist in your area.

ISBN-13: 978-0-373-79571-0

ANOTHER WILD WEDDING NIGHT

Copyright © 2010 by Leslie A. Kelly.

ABOUT THE AUTHOR

Leslie Kelly has written more than two dozen books and novellas for Harlequin Blaze, Harlequin Temptation and HQN Books. Known for her sparkling dialogue, fun characters and depth of emotion, Leslie has been honored with numerous awards, including a National Readers' Choice Award and three nominations for the RWA RITA® Award. Leslie resides in Maryland with her own romantic hero, Bruce, and their three daughters. Visit her online at www.lesliekelly.com.

Books by Leslie Kelly

Don't miss any of our special offers. Write to us at the following address for information on our newest releases.

Harlequin Reader Service
U.S.: 3010 Walden Ave., P.O. Box 1325, Buffalo, NY 14269
Canadian: P.O. Box 609, Fort Erie, Ont. L2A 5X3

To Gina Hayes-McCann.
The greatest cousin anyone could ever ask for...
and my honorary 5th sister!

Prologue

AMANDA BAUER WASN'T VERY big on planning, nor was she too great on details. A big-picture person, she didn't technically fly by the seat of her pants—she was too good a pilot for that. But she usually only cared about crossing every T or dotting every I when those letters were part of a flight plan.

Still, there was one thing she *had* put a lot of thought and planning into: her wedding. So hearing about a screwup with the reservations at the country inn/resort where the members of her wedding party, and eighty guests, were supposed to be staying, didn't make her already-cloudy wedding day shine any brighter.

"Manda, it's not the end of the world," said Reese Campbell, the incredible man she would be marrying in two hours time. He sounded so calm and reasonable, as always. That was one reason he was her perfect man—he made home a place, not just a word, and was her very best friend. "It'll be okay."

"I can just hear my parents now. 'Anyone who would plan a Halloween wedding and expect their guests to come to a costume party afterward should expect nothing but trouble.'"

"Yeah, that sounds like them." He slid an arm around her waist and tugged her close. "But who cares what they think? What day could possibly be better for *us?*"

True. They'd met one year ago. Last Halloween had been the beginning of a wild holiday affair during which she and Reese had indulged in a lot of role-playing fantasy all over the country. They'd fallen in love in the process. So a Halloween-weekend wedding had sounded perfect, and an after-reception costume party even more so. Odd, yes. Unique. But absolutely right for *them* and the way they'd started out.

"Have I told you lately how beautiful you are?" he asked, tipping his head down to brush a soft kiss on her cheek.

"Thank you. But so much for not seeing me before the ceremony," she grumbled, thankful only for the fact that she hadn't been wearing her gown when she'd come down here to have a knock-down drag-out fight with the staff.

When she'd found out the inn had double-booked a quarter of their rooms, meaning several of her guests would be left sharing, or commuting back to the city, she'd almost had a full-on Bridezilla meltdown. Calling Reese had been the only way she could think of to occupy her hands so she wouldn't reach across the reception desk and strangle the chirpy little clerk who'd had the audacity to say it would be "neat" to have some Hollywood people around to lend some glamour to her big day.

She didn't want glamour. She wanted family and romance and fun and a big old party to cap off the night.

But no. A movie crew had invaded this small town an hour outside of Chicago. Here to film a sequence for an action flick, they had practically taken over. It didn't seem to matter that she'd booked the entire inn four months ago. Somebody had fouled up and the L.A. types were already here, ensconced in some of the cottages dotting the grounds, as well as a number of the rooms.

Including the damned bridal suite. Which was currently being occupied by a movie star. *Grr.*

"Mix-up my ass," she muttered. "I'll bet that ditzy clerk saw Ericson's name and sabotaged our reservations on purpose!"

Well, at least Drew Ericson was the leading man, and not a woman. No bride wanted to compete with Angelina Jolie or Megan Fox on her wedding day. Still, she might have trouble keeping her bridesmaids on the job if Ericson happened to come into sight.

"We'll just make the best of it," Reese said, drawing her away from the front desk. Because even Reese, with all his charm, hadn't been able to change the situation. At least he'd gotten a *huge* discount off the bill, though, and payment for rooms at an alternate location twenty miles away. "So a few guests won't get to stay here. You know some will be relieved to have an excuse not to come tonight. Not everybody is looking forward to it."

"Like my parents and the Mannings."

His nose wrinkled, thinking of Amanda's sister, Abby, and her soon-to-be in-laws. "Yeah, sorry, I just can't picture your poor sister's wedding. I'm not surprised she keeps putting it off. She might as well get married at the north pole—her fiancé's family is about that warm."

"Which is why they've become my mom and dad's best friends. The four of them could have been the Snow Miser's grandparents."

She frowned as she thought of Abby, who was engaged to marry a very handsome but aloof attorney. She and her sister hadn't been close for a long time—in fact, Amanda had asked her best friend, Jazz, to be maid of honor, rather than her only sibling. That had just about caused World War III with their mother, but Abby had understood.

In recent months, though, when Abby—who worked as an event planner—had been helping to plan for today, they had grown closer. So she could see that her sister was unhappy; anyone who wasn't totally blind could see it.

Which didn't say much for their parents' eyesight. Or her fiancé's, for that matter.

"Maybe we shouldn't tell Bonnie what's going on," he said.

"Why not?"

"It's a long story."

Bonnie was one of Reese's siblings—and a bridesmaid. Of his four sisters, she was the one with whom Amanda had become the closest. Bonnie had a huge heart. Unfortunately she hadn't found the right guy to share it with. Amanda sensed she wanted that very much, even if everyone else swore she'd had no interest in anything except her causes from the time she was little. A middle child, Bonnie had carved out her niche in the family by always playing peacemaker...but that shouldn't rule out a romantic life, as far as Amanda was concerned.

"I want to hear this story sometime."

"It involves Drew Ericson."

"Ooooh. Is she a rabid stalker-fan?" Amanda asked, not serious.

He snorted a laugh. "Hardly. Can you see Bonnie at a hand-grenade-flinging action flick?"

"Not a chance."

Bonnie had never met a tree she didn't want to hug, and was the most genuine person Amanda had ever met. It wasn't right that someone so beautiful and kind at heart spent her nights alone.

Unfortunately that spending-her-nights-alone thing had been pointed out last night, at the rehearsal dinner. While Bonnie was the peacemaker, the other middle child, Debbie, was a wise-ass, who'd made a snarky remark about her sister's nearly virginal state. Normally passive Bonnie had fried her sister with a glare.

"She was arrested for taking part in a peaceful protest when Drew Ericson was filming a movie last spring," Reese explained.

"Arrested for being *peaceful?*"

"I don't know the details. But she spent a night in jail." He shook his head, as if unable to visualize it any more than Amanda could. "Whatever happened, it left her hating his guts."

Now it was Amanda's turn to snort. "She's incapable of it."

"Okay," Reese conceded, "wrong word. Let's just say if she had to decide who to save from a burning building—Drew Ericson or a lab rat—she'd probably save the rat."

Amanda laughed, as she knew he'd wanted her to. Reese was trying to lighten her mood, and she loved him for it.

"Maybe we should see if Bonnie wants to switch hotels before she finds out he's here," he added.

"She can't. She's in the wedding party. Believe me, if I let Bonnie go, Jazz would be right out the door behind her. I think she'd be thrilled if she got to skip the party, considering I picked out her costume."

"Yeah, I can't wait to see her as a fairy-tale princess."

"Hey, it's her own fault for putting off doing it for so long. And, after all, she told me to just grab her something off-the-rack." And oh, grab she had.

Amanda figured her best friend would look gorgeous no matter what she wore, with her deep, violet eyes and jet-black hair. But since Jazz worked as the lead mechanic at Clear Blue Air, and usually wore either coveralls or jeans and engineer boots, the frilly, feminine costume would definitely be a change.

"So, you're okay? No more worrying?" Reese said.

Nodding, Amanda walked with him across the expansive foyer of the inn—its oak-planked floor gleaming, a faint scent of lemon rising from the freshly polished surface. The management might have fouled up her reservations, but she still loved this gorgeous old mansion, which seemed more like a Southern plantation than an Illinois country house.

"I'm fine," she promised, already moving past the disappointment and anticipating the rest of the day.

Suddenly a voice intruded from above. "What are you doing? You're not supposed to see each other before the wedding!"

Amanda and Reese exchanged a smile as his mother came jogging down the stairs, her curlers bouncing. The woman seemed to love her role as mother-of-the-groom.

"Now, you, scoot! Go put on your tux, then track down your groomsmen and make sure they're presentable," his mother said to Reese. "And you, come on. You've got some champagne to drink, some bridesmaids to giggle with and a beautiful gown to put on."

"I'd rather do that," Reese said. "Well, except the giggling part. And the gown."

"You crazy man." Amanda quickly kissed her groom. "I can't wait to marry you."

"Ditto," he said, his warm, loving smile sending warmth zinging throughout her entire body. "And please don't worry anymore about the rooms, sweetheart. I promise you, this is going to be a night nobody will ever forget."

First Kiss

_1_

BONNIE CAMPBELL WANTED that bouquet.

Everybody who knew her was aware she seldom asked for anything for herself. She would give the last dime out of her wallet to a stranger, would fight for the rights of the oppressed until she had no breath left in her body, and had, in fact, given the shirt off her back to a homeless person.

But she wanted that bouquet.

She'd never caught one. Actually she'd never tried. Not once in her twenty-five years had she gone elbow to elbow with a bunch of desperate women fighting to pluck the promise of marital bliss out of thin air. In fact, she'd felt a little embarrassed for them, sad that women were reduced to such desperate measures, all in the quest for romance.

And yet...she wanted that bouquet.

Which was why she stood in a crowded vestibule at the base of a sweeping staircase, watching her new sister-in-law, Amanda, fling the flowers over her shoulder from far above toward a crowd of single-but-don't-wannabe females.

"Watch out," a woman said, shoving her way to floral glory.

Bonnie watched the flowers arc through the air, heading directly for the bride's sister—who stood just a few feet away. Abby Bauer didn't look pleased about that. In fact, deer-in-headlights best described her expression, as if she hoped she *wouldn't* catch the bouquet as much as Bonnie hoped she *would*.

So she probably wouldn't mind if Bonnie stole it away.

Sending up a little mental apology, she lunged for the prize. Only at the last second, Abby swung her arm out and swatted it like a major league batter swinging at a fastball, sending it in the opposite direction.

"Missed it by that much," Bonnie whispered when the flowers landed in the hands of a bosomy blonde—the kind who'd probably had males flocking around her since she hit puberty.

Bonnie, on the other hand—quiet, petite, curly-haired Bonnie—well, she wasn't sure anybody noticed she'd hit puberty until after she'd graduated from high school.

"I got it!" the blonde shrieked, bouncing around joyfully.

"Hey, what was that all about? I thought you were far too enlightened to get down in the dirt with us competitive she-sharks," an amused voice said. "How much champagne have you had?"

Glancing over her shoulder, she saw her sister, Debbie. Her college-aged sibling had that devilish, I'm-just-waiting-to-find-a-reason-to-make-fun-of-you look on her face. Usually Debbie focused on stirring up everyone else, but last night, she'd turned her wicked sense of humor in Bonnie's direction.

Bonnie still hadn't quite forgiven her for the *almost-*

virgin remark. Not only because everybody at the rehearsal dinner had heard, but because it wasn't too far from the truth.

Which sucked. Badly.

"I'm not drunk," Bonnie said. "I just happen to like tea roses."

"Yeah, right. 'Cause there's no other way to get a bunch of roses than a hair-pulling contest. Come on, what gives?"

"It's not every day our brother gets married," Bonnie said with a shrug, not about to explain *what gave*. Especially because she couldn't explain it without coming across like an idiot.

Debbie rolled her eyes. "Well, as far as I'm concerned, you shouldn't be worrying about catching a bouquet. You don't need to get married. You just need to get laid."

Bonnie frowned, not only at the mouthy comment, but because, again, Debbie was a little too perceptive. Frankly Bonnie hadn't been trying to catch that bouquet due to any white lace dreams. She'd had sexy, black-satin ones in mind, instead. And Debbie's virginal comment had put them there the previous night. Not that she was about to share that little tidbit.

"We'd better move so the guys can try to catch the garter."

She only hoped a certain groomsman didn't catch it.

"You mean so Tom can catch it," Debbie said with a grin.

Uh, yeah. *That* certain groomsman. He had been the reason she, for the first time ever, had almost involved herself in a catfight over a bunch of flowers.

Reese's friend Tom had a reputation as the most successful garter-catcher of his generation. In ancient times, epic poems would have been written about his triumphs in the garter wars.

He was also said to be an equally talented female-catcher. And while there had been no poetry, there were definitely some over-the-top tales circulating about his sexual prowess. Her older sister—divorced and angry—had long called him "the man whore." But Bonnie had only half believed the rumors.

She'd had a crush on him. He'd been every teenage girl's fantasy—the flirtatious older guy who'd teased her mercilessly. Their paths hadn't crossed in a few years, and she'd wondered if he was still as handsome and cocky as ever.

She'd found out at last night's rehearsal. Oh, yeah. Still handsome. Still single. Still cocky.

Still treating her like she was a kid.

That had bothered her. Then, after Debbie's comment, it had *really* bothered her.

God, did everyone in the family think that just because she cared about the environment and the needy, she didn't have a libido? Was she doomed to be Bonnie-the-*nice*-Campbell-girl forever? To always be Bonnie-the-peacemaker, Bonnie-the-bleeding-heart? Just because she'd carved out a place in her huge family by filling that role throughout her childhood didn't mean she hadn't grown up and have a woman's desires.

Okay, maybe she hadn't lived her adult life in a way that would change any opinions. She'd been busy with school, work and volunteering and hadn't had time for any long-term romantic entanglements. She'd never brought a man around to meet the family, never been engaged, never lived with anyone. As far as her family—Debbie—knew, she *could* still be a virgin.

She wasn't, though. Her first lover had been a long-haired guitarist she'd met in college. He'd been a crusader for the legalization of marijuana, for medicinal purposes, he'd said.

Uh…sure. They'd broken up after his third drug bust.

Since then, she'd had a four-month-long relationship with a grad student, before he left to join the Peace Corps. And something resembling a one-night stand.

Pathetic. But she hadn't really thought about *how* pathetic until Debbie's virgin crack.

That's why she'd thought of Tom. Sexy Tom. Tom who knew women, loved women, worshipped women, made pleasuring women his life's mission—or so "they" said.

Maybe he wasn't the dog everyone made him out to be—the stories might have come out of spite or jealousy. But if they were true, well, there were worse people to break a sexual dry spell with than one who was so interested in sex! Maybe the best way to shed her good-girl image was to have sex with a very bad boy.

Either way, getting a little closer to Tom hadn't seemed like such a bad idea. But after he'd done everything but give her noogies on her head last night, she'd realized she had to do something to make him see her as the adult she was now, not his friend's kid sister.

Which brought her to the bouquet. Whoever caught it would have some sexy fun, and share a dance, with whoever caught the garter. If he had to slide a bit of lace all the way up her thigh and couldn't see she had a woman's long legs and a woman's curves, he *never* would.

He never will.

Because she'd blown it. No bouquet. No sexy garter moment for her, just for the stacked blonde. No wedding night fling just to remind herself she was a sensual woman with normal wants, despite what her family, especially her snide little sister, might think.

Nope. Wasn't going to happen. How depressing.

"I'm tired. I'm going to find a place to sit down."

She didn't wait for Debbie to respond. She merely walked away, knowing her sister would be too interested in the garter-toss to follow. She also made a concerted effort to avoid bumping into any of her other siblings— tough since she had five.

Keeping her head down, she skirted the crowd, ignoring everyone, at least until she overheard a snippet of conversation between two of the other guests—both old friends of her mother.

"It is a shame we have to move to another hotel," said one.

"But it couldn't be helped," was the reply.

Bonnie stopped, eyeing the pair. "Excuse me, I couldn't help overhearing. Is there a problem with the rooms?"

"There was a mix-up and some of them were given out to those movie people," one explained.

"*Movie* people?"

The woman nodded.

Yuck. Of all the shallow people she'd ever met, those who lived in Hollywood were the worst. She couldn't believe how callously they treated vulnerable lands and habitats just to make the next blockbuster. From the fur they wore to the exotic animal dinner parties they hosted, she had no use for any of them. Especially since one particular actor had had her tossed into jail last spring, just because she'd tried to stop his crew from damaging the habitat for a rare species of bird.

"Didn't you hear?" the other woman asked. "They're

filming a movie nearby and the cast and crew are staying here." She tittered. "There's even a handsome movie star staying in the bridal suite."

Bonnie's eyes had begun to narrow as soon as she heard "movie people." When "movie star" and "bridal suite" entered the conversation, steam came out of her usually pacifistic ears.

"A spoiled, selfish actor is staying in the bridal suite where Reese and Amanda should be spending their wedding night?"

Nodding, the woman bit her lip, as if realizing that Bonnie—the nicest Campbell kid—was ready to go postal on someone.

Well, not quite that far. But a stern talking-to was definitely in the picture. "I'm going to find Abby, the bride's sister," she told the women, shaking with indignance. "She's the wedding coordinator. She'll do something about this."

And if Abby wouldn't? Bonnie would.

THOUGH THEY WEREN'T HIS favorite part of the job, Drew Ericson didn't usually mind location shoots. True, he hoped he'd never again have to set foot in the small Louisiana town where he'd spent eight hot, miserable weeks last summer shooting a movie about a bayou-born bounty hunter. But in general, since he was single and childless, being away from southern California for weeks at a time wasn't a big deal.

Until now. Because his stalker had followed him here.

"Are you sure it was her?" he asked, talking into his cell phone to one of the production assistants on the film *Grey Steele*—a movie in which he played the mysterious Mr. Steele.

"I'm sure, Mr. Ericson," the younger man said. "We were all given her mug shot so we could watch out for her."

"Hell." Drew glanced around the large suite, noting that the privacy curtains were firmly closed. Considering he had just gotten out of the shower, was still wet and wore only a towel slung around his hips, that was a good thing.

It wasn't that he feared Helen Jarvis. But damn, she was annoying. He was sick to death of feeling like he couldn't take a single step without being watched. The very thought that he now had to check the room every time he entered infuriated him.

The assistant continued. "I spotted her outside the shop where we were shooting today. When she saw me, she took off."

Of course she did. Considering he had a restraining order against her, Jarvis knew better than to stick around and get caught. "Did you let the guards know?"

"Yes, and the local police. Security will be tight."

Good. Though, honestly, he didn't hold out much hope that they'd catch her. The woman was as slippery as Jell-O. Security was tight on movie sets, too…yet she'd once managed to get on the lot and wait for him inside his trailer.

She'd done a lot of crazy things to get close to him—including showing up in his backyard during a private party. The woman even seemed ready to risk bodily injury to get his attention. Once she'd thrown herself in front of his car as he pulled out of his driveway—hoping he'd hit her, and have to stop.

Thank God he had good reflexes. And good brakes.

At first, everyone had laughed it off as part of the biz.

Then she'd shown up at a restaurant where he'd been meeting with his manager, posing as a waitress to take their order. Seeing her crazed desperation firsthand, his manager acknowledged the situation was serious. Like the-David-Letterman-stalker serious.

But the worst moment had been a call from his mother. A strange woman had followed her into a store and introduced herself as his girlfriend. When his mother had reacted with suspicion, the woman had gotten angry.

Harassing his sixty-year-old mother had been the straw that broke this camel's back. There was no more laughing Helen Jarvis off, so he'd brought in the authorities, had her charged with stalking and filed a restraining order. She wasn't supposed to get within five hundred feet of him, his family, or his property.

And yet, she'd still followed him to Illinois.

"Everybody's on alert," the assistant said, "though, maybe if she thinks she's been spotted, she'll get out of town."

Hopefully. But he doubted it—the woman didn't operate that way. Which meant he was again going to have to be on guard for her throughout the next few weeks. "Okay, please let me..."

He was interrupted by a sharp knock on the door to his room. Drew hesitated, the phone still at his ear.

"Sir? Everything okay?" the assistant asked.

"Yeah, sorry," he mumbled. "Keep me posted."

He ended the call and walked quietly toward the door.

Another knock. Harder this time. Sharp and impatient.

Jarvis had never been brazen enough to just knock before. It wasn't her slimy style. Then again, he hadn't seen her since the restraining order. Maybe it had pushed

her over the edge. He just wished she would take no for
an answer—because that's the one he'd given to her on
the few occasions they'd come face-to-face. Then again,
considering he suspected she was nuttier than a bag of
trail mix, that was probably too much to expect.

"Hello? Would you please answer the door, I need to
talk to you!" a woman said.

He hadn't listened closely enough to his stalker to
know her voice, but it sure wasn't anyone else's he recognized. His tension increased, his eyes narrowing as
he stared at the door.

"Look, I heard you talking, I know you're in there.
Stop being such a jerk and open the door."

Jerk? He was a jerk for not wanting a crazy woman
harassing his parents or breaking into his house?

This had gone beyond annoying to infuriating. He
couldn't remember the last time he'd been so angry. Ignoring the advice he'd gotten from the police, he flipped
the lock, grabbed the knob and yanked the door open.

"I've had enough of this! Who the hell do you think
you are?" he snapped, glaring at the woman.

Who *wasn't* Helen Jarvis.

In fact, she looked absolutely nothing like the fortyish
Helen Jarvis, who had bright red hair, bushy eyebrows
and a crazy light in her eyes.

"Oh," he muttered, staring at the extremely attractive
young woman, clad in a long, emerald-green gown.

She looked familiar for some reason, though he
couldn't immediately say why. He just knew the thick,
honey-gold hair tumbling in wavy curls halfway down
her back framed an incredibly pretty face, complete with
sparkling amber-brown eyes and lush lips. She wasn't
very tall, but the formfitting dress revealed some im-
pressive curves. He'd put her in her mid-twenties, a few

years his junior. And she looked every bit as shocked that he'd yanked the door open so abruptly as he was at seeing someone other than the person he expected to find.

The shock quickly dissipated, though.

"Oh, for heaven's sake, it's *you?*" she said, her voice dripping with disdain. "You're the movie star? I can't believe this!"

Drew gaped. The woman who'd been banging on his door, calling him a jerk, was indignant that *he'd* been the one to open it. She'd apparently expected to tell off someone else.

"Go get dressed," she ordered. "I'm not some bimbo. That he-man, muscular look doesn't impress me."

Which was when Drew remembered he wasn't wearing any clothes. Just a white rectangle of terry cloth riding low on his hips, catching the rivulets of moisture that slowly streamed down his body from his wet hair. "Look, I think you have the wrong room," he said, tightening the knotted towel.

"No, *you're* the one who has the wrong room, Mr. Ericson," she shot back. "And if you had any decency, you'd get out of it."

"Who *are* you?"

Her eyes narrowed and her lips pursed in derision. "You don't know?"

"I haven't got a clue," he replied, even as that hint of memory teased his brain.

The answer seemed to annoy her even more. "Of course, you wouldn't, Mr. Movie Star."

Down the hall, the door to another room creaked open a few inches and a pair of nosy eyes peered out. Already on edge from the producer's call, and the stress of dealing with the stalker situation, not to mention this

woman looking at him like she'd scraped him off the
bottom of her shoe, he immediately stiffened.

He had no idea who those eyes belonged to. For all
he knew, Helen Jarvis could be behind that door. Maybe
she'd even arranged for this woman to serve as a distraction to get him to answer.

Whatever the case, standing out here wearing only a
towel, within sight of Jarvis, or a tabloid reporter, or a
member of his fan base, was a really bad idea.

He was just about to close the door in the strange
woman's pretty face when she said, "I should have
known it would be you. Who else would be arrogant
enough to do this?"

"Do what?" he barked, almost shaking with frustration over a conversation that completely confused
him.

"Ruin someone else's wedding, that's what!" She
pointed an index finger at him, stepping closer, until the
soft, satiny fabric of her dress brushed his bare calves,
bringing a quick, surprising rush of awareness. He was
also hit with a hint of a feminine perfume, soft and
pretty. Like her.

Though, right now, she seemed anything but soft.

"I know you actor types are used to getting your own
way, but would it have killed you to be unselfish for
once? A regular room couldn't do for one night?"

The room. She was here to harass him about where
he was staying, not to lay a trap, not to draw his attention away from any crazy stalker who might be lurking nearby, waiting to slip into his bed while he was
distracted.

It was just about the damn room.

Both relieved and very curious, he said, "Sorry, lady,

I don't have private conversations in full view of anyone who wanders by."

Without warning, he reached for her arm and pulled her inside. Drew forced himself to ignore the softness of her skin, or think about how soft the *rest* of her might feel. It had obviously been way too long since he'd had sex if he couldn't stop thinking about how much he'd like to touch every inch of this woman, who'd been practically shouting in his face.

Her mouth had dropped open when he'd touched her, and she shook his hand off the minute she stepped over the threshold. "You can't just go grabbing people like that."

"I can if they're screeching unfair accusations at me in public," he said as he shut the door firmly behind her.

"Oh, yeah, I'm sure you're really concerned about your privacy considering you open doors to strangers when you're half-naked," she said with a definite eye-roll.

"You're a little hung up on me being half-naked," he said, just to egg her on. And, he had to admit, to see if she felt any hint of that spark he'd been feeling since the moment he'd opened the door.

She sputtered, a faint flush of color rising to her cheeks. "Wow, that's some ego. You should really get over yourself. You're not *that* interesting to look at."

People magazine would say differently, but, of course, he didn't point that out. That "Most Beautiful People" list was all kinds of embarrassing—not that he'd ever cracked the Top 10.

"Anyway, I don't care. Do what you want, get dressed or don't. I'm not intimidated."

Calling her bluff, he ignored the clothes strewn on

the bed, strolling over to casually lean against the back
of the couch, which separated the sleeping and sitting
areas of the suite. He didn't bother tightening up the
towel, which had slipped so low, it was now just an inch
or two above his groin—close to the money shot that
would earn him an extra five mil if he ever went there
in a motion picture.

She noticed. Her flush deepened a little; he could see
that from several feet away. She parted her lips to suck
in a deep, calming breath. Her low-cut dress revealed
her slender, delicate throat and he'd swear he could see
the flicker of her pulse pounding harder in her veins.

Or maybe he was just feeling his own.

Because oh, that dress *was* definitely low-cut, that
throat *was* delicate, those curves *were* entirely too distracting. And the heat in her eyes, which she couldn't
completely disguise, was arousing a response in him.
Seriously arousing it.

Cool off, jackass.

He needed to bring down the temperature. Pronto.
Getting hot and bothered about a complete stranger
who'd just called him a selfish jerk and looked like she
hated his guts was not a good way to start the evening.

"Would you like a drink?" he asked, gesturing toward
the minibar.

"No, thank you."

"Suit yourself," he said, grabbing himself a bottle of
water from the fridge.

"Oh. That kind of drink."

He had the feeling she thought he had intended to
ply her with alcohol—him being the big, bad movie
star and despoiler of innocents and all. Without a word,
he reached in, grabbed another bottle and handed it
to her.

Their hands brushed on the cold plastic, just a hint of connection, an air kiss of fingertips. But, just like when he'd grabbed her to haul her inside, he felt the sizzle from his hand all the way up his arm and throughout the rest of his body.

The woman was getting to him. Big-time.

She mumbled her thanks, opened it and took a drink as well. As she did, Drew found himself eyeing her left hand. Force of habit. Unfortunately married women didn't seem to mind cheating so much if it was with a celebrity.

She wore a small ring on the finger in question, but it looked like an opal or pearl. Not very married or engagedish, at least he hoped.

Good.

Though why he immediately thought that a good thing, he didn't know. He might be feeling some major attraction, but she didn't seem to be. He'd met the woman all of five minutes ago, and most of that time, she'd been glaring or snarling at him.

Which, actually, was kinda cute, contrasted to the sweetness of her lovely face and soft lips.

"Now, why don't you start over and tell me what it is I did that has you so furious." He lifted his mouth in a half smile, one that had worked on a lot of heroines in a bunch of movies.

She was either immune, or did a good impersonation of it. Swallowing hard and shaking her head, she said, "You're ruining my brother's wedding."

Wow. Big accusation, since he didn't know her, or her brother. "What do you mean?"

She began to explain the situation, her every word layered with reproach. When he realized the cast and crew of his movie had actually cost a bunch of people with reservations their rooms during someone else's big weekend celebration, he began to understand her anger. In fact, he probably would have felt exactly the same way.

"Look, I'm sorry, I didn't know there was a problem with the reservations. I don't handle these things."

She hesitated, staring hard as if gauging his sincerity. Then her jaw pushed out a little, suspicion and stubbornness quickly returning. "It's not just about the guests' rooms. The wedding actually took place *today*."

"Well, I kinda figured that out. You are wearing a bridesmaid dress. And, unlike most I've seen, it's not an ugly one," he said with a wry grin.

Though, to be honest, the idea of taking that dress off her was looking better by the minute. Now that he knew she wasn't just loco, and had a reason for coming up here and telling him off, he was having a hard time thinking of much else.

Even if she hadn't been wearing the dress, he would have known the ceremony had taken place today. When he'd come back from the set this afternoon, he'd caught sight of an attractive bridal couple who looked blissfully happy.

Curious about that ring, he added, "So, were you the maid of honor? Or the *matron* of honor?"

Kind of a heavy-handed way to ask if she was married, but he was flying by the seat of his pants here.

"Neither," she replied, then tenaciously went back to her point, not answering his real, unasked question. "So, think about it. If the wedding was today, that means that tonight is the wedding night. You follow me?"

"Well, that would make sense." He refrained from making any lascivious wedding-night jokes, sensing that would only piss her off even more.

She waved an arm around, pointing to the silky sheers flowing down over the four-poster bed with its fluffy pillows and plush duvet. Then at the intimate café table with a vase of red roses, the fainting couch and, through the open bathroom door, the oversize bathtub complete with a tile inlaid swan on the wall above it.

"Tell me, did you happen to notice what room you're in?"

"Uh…a nice one?"

Gritting her teeth in visible frustration, she took a deep breath, as if to calm herself, then said, "You're in the honeymoon suite."

A lightbulb clicked on in his brain. "Oh, hell. Your brother and his wife were supposed to have this room for the night."

"Bingo. But they can't. Because a…"

"Don't say it," he said, holding his hand up, palm out. "I've been called a selfish movie star enough for one day, thank you very much."

"If the shoe fits…"

"Hey, I'm a guy, okay? Forgive me for not being smart enough to add bride and groom and honeymoon suite together and realize I needed to give up my room."

Her eyes widened a tiny bit, as if he'd caught her off guard at his willingness to give up his room. He didn't know why, though. It was, of course, exactly what he was going to do.

"You mean you…"

"I'm an actor, not royalty. Believe me, I really don't mind changing rooms. It's not a big deal."

Drew didn't give it another thought. He didn't feel prompted by her accusations or the heat in her eyes. He simply did the right thing. As he always tried to do.

Walking over to the antique desk, he picked up the

phone, called down to the front desk and told them he wanted to switch rooms with the newlyweds'.

And that, for the first time since he'd laid eyes on her, left the sexy stranger in the green dress utterly speechless.

2

AND TO THINK SHE'D ALWAYS considered movie stars predictable creatures. Well, hadn't she been proved wrong.

They were not supposed to be nice, thoughtful and generous unless there was a starving orphan to coo over, an impoverished nation laying laurels at their feet or a camera crew nearby to capture the moment. Nor did they just open their hotel room doors and yank strangers inside, while wearing nothing but a small—*oh, so small*—towel.

So when Drew Ericson—wearing that small, *oh, so small,* towel—called to request a room change, she honestly didn't know what to say. In fact, she couldn't say anything. She could only stare from a few feet away, feeling about as embarrassed as she'd ever felt in her life.

Bonnie—the *nice* Campbell girl—had come in here with a boatload of preconceptions and an attitude a mile wide. She'd called the man names, accused him of all kinds of things, because she was in a pissy mood after not catching a stupid wedding bouquet and facing down a sister who'd called her a virgin.

What was wrong with her? She had gone so far afield from her usual calm, gentle nature, she almost didn't recognize herself. She'd been spoiling for a fight—and Bonnie was the lover of the family, not the fighter.

Of course, part of the blame could probably be laid at the feet of the infamous Drew Ericson. After all, she did owe him a big heaping batch of payback for what he'd done to her last spring. And he didn't even remember!

That so hadn't improved her mood.

"Okay? Am I forgiven now?" the actor asked as he hung up the phone and turned around, a slight smile tickling those impossibly sexy lips.

She suspected his lips had launched the man's career. She didn't think any woman on earth—including already famous female movie stars who had some hand in casting—wouldn't want to sample them at least once.

His mouth wasn't his only devastatingly attractive feature. He had a strong, masculine, square-jawed face to go with it—emphasized by a pair of the bluest eyes she'd ever seen. When combined with his jet-black hair, the man had looks that would stop traffic, even if he weren't famous worldwide.

And then, of course, was the body... *Oh, God, the body.*

She'd lied when she said he wasn't interesting to look at. Because, frankly, only a woman without an ounce of estrogen would *not* want to look at him.

It was a bad thing that she'd had sex on her mind since last night. A very bad thing. Because this man was sex on a stick. Absolutely mouthwatering from his muscular shoulders, to his flexing arms, his broad chest, the muscles rippling across his flat stomach. And down to the edge of that towel. Even his legs and feet were perfect.

She'd seen him from a distance before, of course, as he'd driven by the protestors picketing his movie set last spring—the protestors *she'd* led. But she'd convinced herself he couldn't possibly be as good-looking up close as he was on airbrushed magazine covers, or in his movies—not that she'd ever seen one.

Now, she realized she'd been wrong. He was to die for. It had been all she could do to remain impassive when she'd let her eyes travel over those long ridges of muscle. She could have spent an hour staring at one errant drop of water that trickled from his hair onto his shoulder, sliding down, blazing a visible trail over the planes and valleys of his slick, hard body.

"Do you happen to know what room your brother and his wife are in tonight?" he asked, moving toward the bathroom. He scooped up a pair of jeans off the bed as he passed.

"Uh, yes. It's on the bottom floor, in the east wing, the very last room."

"Okay, thanks. Somebody from the staff is going to let them know, then clean out the room and move me down there," he said, not having shut the door all the way. He'd intentionally left it ajar so he could talk to her from inside the bathroom.

The bathroom with the mirror.

The bathroom with the mirror in which she—*oh, my*—could now see his amazing butt as he dropped the towel to the floor!

Holy crap. Movie star ass. Unbelievable movie star ass. The man could be a butt model, if there was such a thing.

Bonnie swung around to stare at the refrigerator, repeating, *I am not a letch* over and over in her mind just so she wouldn't turn back around for another peek. Of course, all the while, she wondered if *he* had turned around, presenting his other side to the mirror. That very interesting other side.

"Stop it," she told herself, sure the man hadn't just mirror-mooned her on purpose. If he wanted to embarrass her or show off his body, he could have dropped the towel right out here. She'd practically dared him to, saying she didn't find him interesting to look at.

Liar, liar, pants on fire. Well, she wasn't wearing pants, but beneath her gown, her underpants sure felt on the verge of exploding into flames.

"Did you want to do anything before they come up here?"

Do anything? Hmm. That was a loaded question.

Ericson emerged from the bathroom, shirtless, wearing just the jeans. She hadn't noticed whether or not he'd grabbed anything to wear under them.

Stop thinking about what he might be wearing under them.

"Hello?"

Trying to pull two thoughts together in her brain, she mumbled, "Huh?"

"After I pack up my stuff, the manager's going to send someone up to move it, then get the room ready for the newlyweds. But if you want to do anything, leave a note or some flowers or something, you could do that now."

Licking her lips, Bonnie said, "Yes, sure, that's a great idea. I'll talk to the wedding coordinator and have some champagne sent up for tonight after the party."

"Is the reception still going on?" he asked, sounding surprised. Then he tsked. "You snuck out of your own brother's wedding reception just to tell me off?"

"No, the official stuff is over. There's a big costume party tonight, though, out in the barn."

He shrugged. "Makes sense, I guess. Convenient that they got married the night before Halloween."

"You'd have to know Reese and Amanda. The party is perfect for them."

"Sounds like fun. Way better than the typical boring wedding reception with a smarmy deejay playing the 'Chicken Dance' and the 'Electric Slide.'"

Sighing, she admitted, "That was this afternoon."

He threw his head back and barked a laugh.

"Something tells me the Hollywood weddings you attend don't have quite the same level of entertainment," she said.

"No, they usually have some once-famous, now slightly has-been band that charges a quarter of a million bucks for a three-hour performance playing the 'Chicken Dance' and the 'Electric Slide.' With a cheesy rendition of 'Daddy's Little Girl' thrown in just for the hell of it."

She couldn't stop a tiny smile from widening her lips. So far, the man was so unlike the image she'd built him up to be in her mind for the past six months. Easy to talk to, quick to smile, laid-back and friendly. Not at all the monster she'd been imagining.

And hot. So damned hot. She wished he'd put a shirt on just so she could stop wondering how those ridges of muscle on his abdomen would feel pressed against her bare stomach.

Or, to be honest, how his bare anything would feel against her bare anything.

"I can't say going to weddings is my favorite thing," he admitted, "so I wasn't too heartbroken about not being invited to Charlie Sheen's latest walk down the aisle."

She chuckled, liking his down-to-earth manner.

Wrong. He's an actor. He could just be playing the role of nice guy. She knew better than most that he wasn't Mr. Friendly.

She stiffened her spine, determined not to be charmed by him. "Let's just say tonight's the real reception—the one that most suits the bride and groom," she said, thinking of how brazen and fun Amanda was—and how much Reese adored her. Then, remembering what he'd said earlier, she added, "And I didn't come up here to tell you off."

"You did a really good impersonation of it."

"Yeah. Sorry."

"What was that? I didn't quite hear you." A grin lingered on those lips and his eyes twinkled. The man was teasing her, knowing he'd firmly put her in her place and had kept her off balance throughout this whole conversation.

But he'd done something very nice that deserved a genuine expression of gratitude, not a grudging, mumbled one. "I'm sorry I was such a basket case. Thank you, Mr. Ericson. I'm sure Reese and Amanda will be truly grateful."

"Drew," he told her, retrieving a long-sleeved Henley shirt from the bed and pulling it on. "You never told me your name."

"It's Bonnie Campbell."

Now fully dressed—*thank God*—he stepped over and extended a hand. "Nice to meet you."

She should have taken the hand and left it at that. Instead she muttered, "We've met before."

His eyes narrowed as he studied her. "You do look

familiar, but I'm sorry, I can't remember why. Were you an extra or something?"

"A what?"

"I mean, did you appear in a scene in one of my movies?"

She snorted. "Definitely not. I would never watch one of your movies, and I most certainly would never appear in one."

The minute the words left her mouth, she realized how rude they sounded. Then again, considering he'd had her arrested, just because she'd wanted to save a bird habitat being damaged by one of his location shoots, he deserved a little rudeness.

But not after the nice thing he did for Reese and Amanda.

Almost stumbling over her words, she hurried to add, "I mean, I'm no actress."

He wasn't fooled. "I don't think not being an actress was your main objection. What's wrong with my movies?"

She couldn't imagine he cared, since he produced blockbuster after blockbuster. So she answered honestly. "They're just not my thing. Too violent, too bloody."

"You're a chick flick fan, huh?"

"Actually, I like nature films." She shrugged in self-deprecation. "And Disney movies. What can I say? I'm a wimp."

"Nature and Disney. Yeah, I can see how Bambi would appeal to someone who abhors violence," he said with a wry look.

Though she sensed he was teasing, she answered seriously. "I can't watch that one."

"Bet *The Lion King*'s not on your best-of list, either."

"Nope."

"Didn't Tarzan's parents get eaten by…"

"Enough!" she snapped. "I get the point."

"But we didn't even start on Cruella de Vil."

Seeing the twinkle in his eyes, she couldn't help chuckling. "Imagine what your adoring public would think if they knew you were such a dweeb."

As soon as the words left her mouth, she bit her lip, having no idea what had come over her. Bonnie had never in her life slung insults at a stranger like that. Though, to be honest, she hadn't been trying to be nasty.

It was just…he'd been very cute when exposing his thorough knowledge of kids movies. She didn't remember ever reading that he had any munchkins of his own, so maybe he was just a soft touch underneath all that rugged, tough-guy swagger. Considering he'd given up his opulent suite for a small, standard room, she suspected that was at least a little bit true.

He drew a hand to his chest. "I'm offended. I thought most guys would get points for being so well-versed on the important cartoon classics of the twentieth century."

She had to give it to him, the guy was charming. Not movie star, schmoozy charming, but genuine and almost boyish. It was an unexpected trait in a guy who made movies that featured weapons and fifteen-minute fight scenes with slow-mo close-ups of blood splattering, at least, so she'd heard. She could probably like this man, if she let herself.

She couldn't let herself, however. Because she was already too attracted to him. Liking might just shove her over the top and have her doing something crazy like asking him if he wanted to shove a lacy garter up her leg.

Or, um, shove something up something.

Stop it, idiot!

"Now, back to the point. Where have we met before?"

She was tempted to just leave without answering, but some part of her—probably the part that still smarted over the fact that she now had an arrest on her record—had to reply. "You probably saw my face through the bars as I was being hauled off your movie set in a paddy wagon."

Exaggeration. But he was an actor—they were used to it.

His impossibly blue eyes widened in shock. "What?"

"You remember the little problem on the set of the Civil War movie you made in Gettysburg last spring?"

He hesitated, then sucked in a shocked breath. Stepping closer, he lifted a hand to her chin and looked straight at her face. "I get it. You were one of those protestors, I definitely noticed you." He nodded slowly, almost smiling. "It took me a while to remember you without the signs. Still, I should have recognized the pissed-off expression, which always seemed so out of place on your beautiful face."

She jerked her chin away, also shoving away the flash of warmth that his words sent rushing through her. *Beautiful?* Hardly. She'd cop to pretty. But she was nowhere near as beautiful as the women he interacted with on a daily basis.

"I can't believe I didn't figure it out sooner."

"Maybe I should have shown up in my prison jumpsuit, that might have jogged your memory."

"Excuse me?"

She told herself to stop exaggerating; there had been

no jumpsuit. "The one they *could* have put me in once you had me hauled off to jail."

"What are you talking about?"

"It doesn't matter anymore, Mr. Ericson. I managed to survive my incarceration. Fortunately my cell-mate was just a tired old prostitute named Sally, not a huge, chain-wearing alpha-dog named Bertha looking to make me her bitch."

He started to laugh, shaking his head as if he thought she'd put one over on him. When she didn't join in his amusement, he said, "You're serious?"

"As if you didn't know."

"I *didn't* know."

Yeah, right. "Forget it. It doesn't matter. Now, if you'll excuse me, I should go."

He put a hand on her shoulder, stopping her from spinning around and walking out of the room. The warm pressure of his strong fingers against her bare skin set those banked sparks of awareness ablaze, until they roared through her. It was an innocent touch, not rough, not aggressive, certainly not sexual. Yet she felt utterly engulfed by the inferno of her own instinctive reaction.

There was power in those hands. Just as much as in the mouth, the face, the amazing body and that captivating personality.

But not a scary power. No, an utterly seductive, fascinating one. She could so easily see herself falling under his spell. And part of her wanted to. Desperately.

Maybe if he weren't a celebrity, if he were just a normal guy—if he hadn't had her tossed into jail—she'd have given in to her incredible reaction to him and taken a shot. But he was nowhere near a normal guy. He was totally out of her league. This wasn't like hoping to hook up with her brother's old friend. This guy was a super-stud who had women at his feet. No way would he be interested in her, and no way would she humiliate herself any more by making her interest known to him. She'd already had her fill of playing Bonnie-the-idiot for one weekend.

"Look, all I remember was there were some protestors who didn't want us filming in the battlefield, even after we'd gotten permission."

"Nobody was upset that you were filming in the battlefield," she clarified. "We were concerned about a rare species of bird that nests in one area of it, and your crew didn't much seem to care about disturbing them during mating season. When I went to try to talk to you about it, I got arrested."

He dropped his hand—*thank God, now breathe*—his frown deepening. "Did you sneak onto the set? Were you near my trailer?"

That made her try to mentally douse the fire. Indignant, she replied, "I didn't 'sneak' anywhere! I nicely asked a sympathetic staff member to take me to somebody in charge. He said you were a good guy and that you liked animals, so you might listen."

"I do," he mumbled. "I would have."

She continued as if he hadn't spoken. "Once I was inside, the guy went to find you, and the next thing you know, I'm grabbed by a guard and accused of being some kind of stalker."

"Uh-oh."

She rolled her eyes. "Jeez, it's not like we were causing any real problems, blocking the driveway or interrupting the filming. All we did was hold up some signs, and for that, I got a trip in the back of a squad car to the local jail."

He swiped a hand through his thick, still-damp hair, leaving it sticking up in jagged, sexy spikes. "Hell."

"Not quite, just a cell. But close enough, thanks." Another exaggeration. The jail actually hadn't been too horrid—it was the embarrassment that had lingered, not any discomfort. But keeping up the attitude helped to remind her she could not, under any circumstances, reach up and sink her own fingers into that messy hair to straighten it out.

Or to tug him close to any part of her body he'd care to sample.

"Bonnie, you have to understand…"

"Oh, I understand. You had a movie to make, and didn't want to deal with protestors trying to save the lives of some silly little birds. So you took care of the problem by having their leader hauled off in handcuffs."

He reached for her hands, lifting them and studying her wrists, as if the cuffs might have left a mark that lingered after all these months.

Bonnie shivered. God, this was almost worse than the touch on her shoulder. Because it was far too easy to imagine him encircling her wrists in those big hands, lifting her arms above her body so she was helpless to do anything but lie there, *loving* it as he made love to her.

"I am so sorry." Surprisingly he sounded truly remorseful.

Swallowing hard, she forced herself to focus, thinking about the words, not the *Penthouse* forum moment taking place in her mind.

"I mean it, I am genuinely sorry, Bonnie."

Well, maybe he was, now that she'd become a real person, not just a nameless protestor he'd been trying to get rid of. During her career in social work, and her volunteerism for social and environmental causes, she'd learned that most people would easily ignore an anonymous voice saying something they didn't want to hear. But when the words came from someone they knew, someone they could put a face and name to, they were more inclined to listen. Apparently she'd become human to the spoiled movie star.

Spoiled—but nice—movie star, she clarified.

"Please forgive me," he said. "And let me explain."

He continued to hold her wrists. That übersexy crazy awareness still sliding through her, Bonnie wondered if he felt her pulse race at the connection even as she pulled away.

"It's okay," she said with a forced shrug. "There's really no need." She began to edge toward the door, knowing she should get out of here, now, before she let herself be any further charmed by the man. Before she could ask him to move those hands somewhere else on her body.

This isn't some guy you can pick up for the night. You did what you came to do, now get out of here.

"You've made up for it by giving up the room to Reese and Amanda," she added, trying so hard to sound appreciative and not lustful. "Thank you."

"You don't understand. Please, sit down, talk to me. I think we've gotten off on the wrong foot here."

"Actually we got off on the wrong foot six months ago."

"So can we start over?"

She scrunched her brow, truly not understanding why he cared. He seemed to want to make things right.

But there was no need. They would never see each other again. She was a tiny little fly who would get splattered on the windshield of his life if she even thought about sticking around any longer. Because as nice as he seemed to be, there was no way he'd be interested in her the way she was becoming more and more interested in him. He could have sex with some of the most beautiful women of their generation. He sure wouldn't want a nearly virginal social worker from Pittsburgh.

"It doesn't matter anymore."

"But I want you to…"

Before he could continue, someone knocked on the door. "Mr. Ericson? I've come to move your bags."

The bags he hadn't even started to pack. They sure did hop to it around here when a superstar gave the orders.

Bonnie didn't mind, though, because the interruption gave her the chance to end this disturbing conversation. She'd come up here furious and righteously indignant at an arrogant actor, and had ended up becoming breathless and far too aware of Drew Ericson as a man. It was like sleeping with the enemy.

Don't even *go there.*

No, she couldn't possibly go there anymore, not even in the darkest, most wicked corners of her mind. Drew Ericson was totally and completely out of bounds. And needed to get totally and completely out of her mind.

Which meant it was definitely time to go.

OVER THE NEXT FEW HOURS, after he'd killed some time in the small lounge area, then moved to his new room, Drew couldn't stop thinking about Bonnie Campbell. If the beautiful young woman were to be believed, she had spent a night in jail, all because of him. Well, him and Helen Jarvis.

"Damn," he said aloud, not for the first time.

Last spring, when he'd gone to Pennsylvania to film

that movie, he'd been fresh off Jarvis's blitz attack in his trailer on the set in California. His manager had raised hell with the studio, and they'd been promised that security would be much tighter in the future, including on location.

It was easy to see what had happened. Bonnie— beautiful, passionate Bonnie—had been mistaken for Helen Jarvis, or someone like her, and had paid the price for the other woman's crimes.

He hadn't known, hadn't really been responsible, but he still felt guilty about it. If only she'd let him explain. But he wouldn't have that chance. She was only here for another day or two, at the most, and he'd be stuck for a few more weeks. Their paths would probably never cross again.

Funny how much that disappointed him, considering he'd only just met the woman. But the brief time he'd spent in her company had delighted him. Bonnie had no artifice—there wasn't a false bone in her body. Coming from a place where everything from smiles to teeth to breasts to personalities were fake, he found that incredibly refreshing. And aside from that, she was a damned beautiful woman. One who'd affected him so deeply, he couldn't stop thinking about her—the softness of her skin, the gleam of gold in her hair, the passion of her voice, the womanly curves of her body.

"The womanly curves you're never gonna see again," he reminded himself.

Disappointment weighing heavily on his shoulders, he finally thought about dinner and reached for the phone to call room service. But before he could dial, someone knocked on the door to his new room—which was smaller than his previous one, but still perfectly comfortable. Even for a spoiled movie star.

He hesitated, waiting to see if his visitor on the other side of the door accused him of being a selfish jerk, or gave any other sign that it was the one person he'd like to see right now.

Silence. Bummer.

This time, though fully dressed, he reacted cautiously as he approached the door. "Yes?"

"Mr. Ericson?"

A man's voice. Good on the one hand—it wasn't Helen Jarvis. Bad on the other—it wasn't Bonnie, either.

"Sorry to bother you. I'm the guy you gave your room to. My wife and I were wondering if we could have a word?"

He heard a feminine laugh at the word wife, and realized the bride and groom were paying him a visit. Not Bonnie—her brother.

Opening the door, he smiled at the couple. They had changed out of their wedding finery, but still shone with happiness that would scream "newlyweds" to anyone who looked at them.

"Hi," he said. "Did you forget something? Come on in."

Rather than responding, the bride—a pretty blonde— rose on tiptoe and kissed Drew's cheek. "Thank you so much."

Her husband smiled, not the least bit concerned. He was obviously confident in his new wife's feelings for him. "I'm Reese Campbell, this is my wife, Amanda. We really appreciate you giving us your room, especially since you've been in it all week, and you'll have to move again once we're gone. It was a nice thing to do."

Drew shrugged. "It's no big deal. I'm just glad I found out about it in time. I would have hated the thought of cheating you out of the bridal suite on your wedding night."

"How *did* you find out?" Reese Campbell asked.

"From your sister."

The other man sighed. "I have four. Care to narrow it down?"

Four? Four like Bonnie? Good God. "It was Bonnie. She came to my room and, uh…made her case."

Reese coughed into his fist, obviously taken by surprise.

His wife seemed even more so. *"Bonnie?"* She eyed her husband. "Lab rat, huh?"

"Excuse me?" Drew asked.

"He told me Bonnie preferred lab rats to you." As if suddenly remembering who she was talking to, she gasped. "I'm sorry. I think I've had a bit too much champagne."

So, Bonnie Campbell thought he was worse than a rat. Considering she believed he'd intentionally had her arrested, he could see why.

"That's okay," he said. "There was a misunderstanding the first time we met. But I think maybe today I went up in her estimation, at least as high as, I dunno…field mouse?"

"Well," said Amanda, her voice ringing with sincerity, "in our estimation, you went straight up to really nice guy."

"I'm glad to hear it. Hope you have a great time tonight."

That had sounded a little cheesy. *Have a great time having wild, steamy sex tonight.* So he quickly added, "I mean, at your costume party. It sounds like a lot of fun."

"I'm sure it will be," Reese said, a twinkle in his

eye saying he'd caught Drew's meaning the first time. "You're welcome to join us, if you'd like. You don't even have to wear a costume."

His wife looked at him like he'd grown two heads. "Yeah, right. The guy who goes to the *Vanity Fair* after-Oscar party wants to hang out with us and our friends and families."

Families. As in *sisters.* Hmm. "Actually I'd be delighted to go," he replied.

The bride's jaw fell open. "Uh…seriously?"

"Yeah. Bonnie will be there, right?"

Reece eyed Drew speculatively. "Of course. Why?"

"I don't know. Maybe I'd like the chance to go from field mouse all the way up to hamster or something."

His wife giggled, but Reese Campbell just continued to stare, his eyes assessing, curious. The protective older brother, wondering if big-bad-movie-star had designs on his sister.

Well, he did. But not in the way Reese Campbell might think. Drew wanted to spend some more time with Bonnie so he could convince her he wasn't the slimeball—er, what was lower than a lab rat?—she thought him to be. And, well, okay, maybe to see if she felt any of the same attraction he felt for her.

She does.

He knew women. He had seen the way her cheeks had pinkened, and how she kept moistening her lips. He'd heard her choppy breaths and felt her racing pulse. She definitely felt something.

Reese must not have seen any ulterior motives in Drew's expression, because he finally began to smile, too. "I tell you what. We'll warn everyone not to harass you, and we'll assign Bonnie to be your bodyguard to make sure of it, okay?"

Pretty Bonnie the bodyguard. He liked the idea. A lot.

Drew stuck out his hand, and Reese took it. As they exchanged a strong, solid shake, Bonnie's brother added, "Just be warned. My sister isn't always the sweet, quiet little bleeding heart she seems to be."

Drew barked a laugh. *Sweet? Quiet?* Yeah. Right. If this afternoon was Bonnie being sweet and quiet, he wondered what she would do when she was furious, or, when she was excited.

Frankly he was really looking forward to finding out…especially about the excited part.

3

"EXCUSE ME?" BONNIE ASKED, not sure she'd heard properly. Her brother *couldn't* have just said what she thought he had.

Reese explained it again. "Drew Ericson is coming to the party—he should be here soon. I told him you'd run interference between him and anybody who gets a little overzealous."

That's what she thought he'd said. "You must be kidding."

He ignored her shock. "Amanda and I have already been spreading the word to everyone to respect the man and let him enjoy himself. But just in case, we figured it would be good for somebody to stick close to him. Since you've already met…"

"Oh, yeah, we've met," she snapped.

"And you didn't like him?" her brother asked, looking curious. "Because I got the feeling he liked you."

"That's ridiculous," she said, even as warmth rose in her face at the very thought of it. Because she had more than liked him. She had wanted the man like she'd never wanted anything in her entire life. Liking hadn't even entered the equation—even if she had begun to suspect she could like him, if she'd allow herself to. "He had me tossed into jail."

One of his brows went up. "Really? He *personally* did that?"

"I think he set the whole thing up," she said, intentionally sticking to her long-held resentment of Drew Ericson. It was her only defense against sheer, utter attraction.

"The guy doesn't make his own hotel reservations. You really think he schemes to get people hauled off to jail?"

Bonnie hesitated, Reese's words sparking a few unexpected thoughts. She'd been angry—furious—for six months. She wasn't accustomed to feeling that way, and had almost needed someone to focus all that anger on. Drew Ericson had fit the bill.

She'd put it all together in her mind long ago, figuring Ericson had gotten someone to let her onto the lot in order to entrap her and get her arrested. No more leader, no more protest.

But what if that scenario wasn't true? As Reese had hinted, Ericson had handlers for everything. He hadn't even noticed he was in a honeymoon suite, for heaven's sake. He had been incredibly contrite, not to mention thoughtful and considerate…and, oh, yeah, just about the sexiest thing on two legs this afternoon.

Was it possible he really wasn't to blame, as she'd assumed all these months?

There was only one way to find out—she had to ask the man.

And when he walked into the party a short time later, and their eyes met across the room, she knew the time had come.

Ignoring the whispers, plus some dreamy sighs—only

a few of which were her own—Bonnie walked toward the entrance. Drew was shaking hands with Amanda and Reese, appearing relaxed and comfortable in the crowd.

"I see you made it," she said.

"He even came up with a costume," said Amanda. She waved at Ericson's clothes—khaki pants, a leather bomber jacket and a brown, broad-brimmed hat.

He looked incredibly handsome, the outfit casually sexy. Masculine. Her fingertips curling into the fabric of her dress, she pictured rubbing them against the soft, worn leather of the jacket, stroking those broad shoulders.

Even more devastating, those intense blue eyes were fixed totally on her. He swept a long, thorough stare over her, from her head, down her long, flowing dress, to her feet.

She was dressed as Mother Nature, and had made the costume herself. Green vines wound through her long hair, and she'd used face paint to draw more on her skin—from her temple, down her cheek, all the way to her neck. The long, low-cut dress was made of soft layers of moss-green fabric that shifted and flowed with every move she made. It whispered around her, like a breeze, and made her feel utterly feminine.

"I like your costume," Drew said in a throaty voice.

Bonnie quivered. Never had she been more aware that the beautiful green fabric she'd used to make the dress was very thin. She'd wanted it wispy and fragile, and it skimmed over her body hugging every bump, curve or nipple it tried to cover.

Nipple? For God's sake, don't think of your nipples.

Too late. It didn't matter if she thought of them or

not. She could already feel the way the material scraped over her puckered, sensitive skin. She told herself it was because she was standing by the door and there was a cool breeze. In truth, she knew she could be standing by a bonfire and her body would react the same way. Because the sexiest man she'd ever seen was staring at her with stark appreciation, and she couldn't have been more aware of him if he stroked her breast right here in front of everyone.

"You do look beautiful, Bonnie," said Amanda.

"Beautiful," Drew repeated.

"Thank you. Uh, your costume is great, too, especially on such short notice." True. He looked incredibly hot. But he *didn't* look like he'd come in costume. "I'm afraid I don't get it, though. Who are you supposed to be?"

Reese frowned at Drew. "Even *you've* heard of Indiana Jones."

"I doubt it," said Drew. "I don't think he's been immortalized in cartoon form yet."

"She might recognize the LEGO-video game version."

Oh, perfect. Her brother and a movie star were ganging up on her. "I know who Indiana Jones is," she said. "I just didn't make the connection."

"Knock it off," said her new sister-in-law. "No picking on Bonnie. The world needs more people like her— with huge, loving hearts." Amanda lifted her champagne glass in salute. "Here's to you, little sister."

"Sorry for making fun of you," said Reese, squeezing her arm. "Now, go play babysitter for Mr. Ericson here, and make sure Great-Aunt Jean doesn't plop down on his lap and ask him how he likes women with a little more experience."

That would be very funny, if it weren't such a possibility. Or if Bonnie wasn't suddenly picturing *herself* plopping down on his lap and asking how he liked women with a little *less* experience.

"Shall we?" she asked.

"Absolutely."

He followed her, stopping every two feet to allow her to make brief introductions, hearing the same sentence again, and again…and again. *I just love your movies!*

A few of the single women tried to say more. That included the blonde who'd caught the bouquet. Strange, Bonnie had figured she would be in a dark corner with Tom by now. Instead she was right here, cooing and tugging at her French maid costume so it slipped a little lower on her more than ample breasts.

Funny, that was the first time she'd thought of Tom since she'd left the reception. Now she wasn't even interested enough to look around the barn and see if he was here, though she wasn't entirely sure why. A few hours ago, it had seemed so important to get his attention today. Now? Not even a little bit.

She didn't allow herself to think it was because of the man standing beside her, the man who charmed every person he met. That was a mental road she wasn't ready to go down. Normal girls from Pittsburgh did not end up with super-stud movie stars. Period.

To give him credit, Drew didn't seem the least bit bothered by the attention. Not a hint of impatience entered his voice as he spoke to person after person. Finally, though, Bonnie's patience started to wear thin. Especially once her youngest sister, Molly, and two of her giggly teenage friends circled him. They resembled a trio of Girl Scouts around a campfire—eyeing him like he was a big marshmallow they wanted to smoosh between their graham crackers.

"I can't believe you're really here!" one of them said.

"Would you *please* say the line from that movie..."

"Okay, that's enough," Bonnie said with a weary sigh. "How about we let Mr. Ericson sit down and have a drink."

Molly wrinkled her nose. "Who made you his babysitter?"

"Actually the bride and groom did," said Drew with a self-deprecating shrug. "I gotta do what she tells me. What can I say? I'm completely at her mercy."

The words rolled off his tongue with the slightest hint of suggestion, and Bonnie watched all three of the girls melt at the thought.

"Let's go," she muttered, grabbing his arm. As she pulled him away, she added, "You'd better steer clear of that redhead. I've known her since she was four and let me tell you, if you're not careful, she'll soon be reenacting that movie *The Crush* with you playing the Cary Elwes part."

"Yikes," he said as they skirted through the room, heading for a table in a back corner. "Is that the creepy one with Alicia Silverstone stalking the single guy?"

"Uh-huh."

He cleared his throat, all wide-eyed innocence as he said, "Thought you only watched cartoons."

Oh, man. She had totally asked for that one. "What can I say? I was a moody adolescent."

Laughing, he replied, "I'm sorry, I was just teasing you again."

Bonnie suddenly stopped, realizing something. She liked this man's laugh. Liked his smile. Liked his sense of humor. Liked the tingle of excitement she felt when he teased her.

Hell, it was too late. She liked Drew Ericson. A *lot*.

This wasn't supposed to happen. How could she like a guy she'd so totally *dis*liked for the past six months? Especially one every other woman in the world had the hots for?

One you have the hots for, too. Admit it.

She might be a wimp when it came to movies, but Bonnie Campbell was not a liar. She could admit it…if only to herself. She did have the hots for this guy. The steamy, boiling hots. She'd gone back to her room after leaving him this afternoon and had seriously considered making friends with the showerhead, that's how hot he'd made her.

"Okay," he said, oblivious to her naughty self-evaluation as they sat at an empty table. "Who else should I worry about tonight?"

Forcing herself to put those crazy ideas out of her mind, Bonnie tapped her finger on her cheek, giving it some thought. "That blonde in the French maid costume caught the bouquet at the reception." *Grr.* "She's on the lookout for a husband tonight."

He grimaced. "That's enough to scare any man. What about this Great-Aunt Jean?"

Glancing around, Bonnie nodded toward her relative, who wore a Queen Elizabeth ensemble, compete with ruff and red wig. "That's her." The woman was holding court among the older guests, all of whom looked to be laughing and having a great time.

Frankly Bonnie hadn't been sure how this whole costume party thing would go over with that generation. She needn't have worried. They appeared to be loving it.

All in all, tonight had proven to be a great success.

The barn was huge, yet still felt bursting at the seams—as if more people were here now than had been at the reception earlier. Considering Reese and Amanda were so happy they'd invited every person they bumped into to come, that was probably not far from the truth.

"She's very imposing," Drew said.

"Aunt Jean? She's a pussycat. Just be warned, she is the nosiest person on the planet. If she gets you alone, she'll ask you all kinds of personal questions."

"Oh? Like what?"

She opened her mouth to respond before noticing his tone had been *too* innocent. The man was good. He'd almost gotten her to answer him, which would have caused her no end of embarrassment once she got started. Because knowing Aunt Jean, she'd ask things like, *What kind of women do you like? Are you seeing anyone? What's it like filming those naughty love scenes?*

The laughter lurking on his mouth confirmed he'd been trying to lead her into saying something she'd regret. "Forget I asked."

"Behave, or I'll abandon you to the marriage-minded maid."

Before he could respond, a man dressed all in black approached the table. Bonnie tried to do her job and say "No autographs," when he pointed out the coat on the back of Drew's chair.

"Oh, sorry," Drew said, standing and passing the coat over.

"Wow, guess he didn't recognize you," she said when they were again alone. "Is that an ego-killer?"

"Are you kidding? It's nice to be incognito for a while."

"Hi, Mr. Ericson! I'm a big fan," a voice said.

So much for incognito.

The fan turned out to be a waiter, dressed in a phantom costume. He was carrying a tray loaded with both champagne glasses and beer bottles. "Would you like something to drink?"

"I'd love a beer," Drew said. After accepting the bottle, he glanced at the label. "Campbell's Lager. Never heard of it."

"It's a family favorite," Bonnie said, not explaining why it was the only brew being served at this particular party.

After sipping, he nodded in appreciation. "Good stuff."

"Glad you like it," she said. "My family owns the brewery."

His brow shot up. "Seriously?"

She nodded. "My grandfather founded it and my father built it into a major East Coast operation." Feeling wistful, as she always did when thinking of her father, who'd died three years ago, she cleared her throat. "Reese is in charge now."

He held up the bottle, sipping again. "This is excellent."

"We're not on the West Coast yet, but give Reese time."

"I'm going to have to ship a few cases back home."

"I'm sure he'd be happy to send you some as a thank-you."

"Hey, I'll buy it by the truckload. Then I'll be the envy of my friends who will want to know where I found it. That'll get some word of mouth going before you break into the California market."

She saw by his expression that he meant it. It wasn't a casual promise, easily offered, easily forgotten. He was genuine and thoughtful. Considerate. And so unlike what she expected.

Which prompted her to finally broach the subject that had been bugging her all day. "So. About having me arrested…"

Drew reached across the table and dropped a hand over hers. Bonnie didn't draw away, surprised by the warm, casual possession of the gesture. Surprised, and also pleased.

"I am so sorry. I've been thinking it over and I think you were probably mistaken for a woman who's been stalking me."

"You mean *all* the women who stalk you?" she asked, enjoying the way that hand felt, heavy and strong on top of hers.

"No, I mean one in particular." His eyes narrowed and frown lines tugged at his brow. For the first time, the laid-back, casual good humor he'd displayed from the moment they'd met seemed to dissipate. "It's a long story."

"I'm listening."

"Okay," he said. "You asked for it."

Yes, she had. So Bonnie remained silent as he told her about this woman, Helen Jarvis, who had taken "crazed fan" up to a whole new level. She supposed it wasn't too surprising that male celebrities were stalked as much as female ones, but she hadn't given it much thought before. Drew was so strong, larger-than-life, it was difficult to imagine how hard it must be to feel helpless to protect his own privacy from someone determined to invade it.

Hearing that the woman had thrown herself in front of his car was bad enough. Then it just got worse.

She gasped. "You're serious? She confronted your mother?"

"Yeah. That was the line in the sand for me."

"I'm not surprised." She cast a quick look across the party toward her own mother, who stood laughing with Aunt Jean. Bonnie and all her siblings had been very protective of their mom since their father's untimely death. She couldn't think of anything they wouldn't do to protect her if she were being threatened.

"The rest was petty garbage—sneaking onto the set, breaking into my trailer, showing up at my house. Going after my family took things too far. That's when I got a restraining order."

Sucking in a breath, Bonnie zoned in on one key part of what he'd said. This crazed woman who'd made his life a nightmare for the past year had snuck onto one of his movie sets. "Oh, God, *that's* why security went nuts when I got on your set!"

"That's why. I wish I knew who it was who brought you in and then abandoned you to get accused of trespassing."

"You and me both," she said. Remembering the very nice young man, she mused, "I bet he was afraid for his job once he saw what had happened. That's probably why he didn't come forward."

"It was a coward's move," Drew said, his mouth tightening.

But even as his tension increased, her own completely disappeared. She suddenly felt as though someone had lifted an enormous weight off her shoulders. Bonnie hadn't really thought about how much the incident last spring had weighed on her, yet it obviously had. She'd felt not only abused and indignant, but actually offended at the thought that she'd been set up.

Now she knew she hadn't been. She had no doubt Drew was telling her the truth. That, more than anything, suddenly made her heart feel lighter than it had in ages. "Thanks for confiding in me," she said, smiling broadly at him, holding nothing back. It was the first real, heartfelt smile she'd offered the man.

Staring into her face for a long moment, he answered, "Thanks for listening. Now, do you think we could start over?"

"As in, pretend I didn't practically bang your door down and accuse you of all kinds of hateful things?" she whispered, overwhelmed with remorse for her own behavior.

He didn't answer. Instead he pushed his chair back and rose to his feet, extending his hand to her. "Will you dance with me?"

She didn't have to give it a second thought. "I'd love to."

HE WAS IN TROUBLE.

Drew had been highly interested in Bonnie Campbell when she'd been a pretty bridesmaid knocking on his door to tell him off. That interest had grown when they'd talked, when he'd learned more about her, heard her laugh, seen that smile.

Now, though, brushing up against her body on the dance floor—feeling the glide of her thigh against his, or the scrape of those perfect breasts against his chest—he had gone from interested to captivated.

He was surrounded by women daily. Most of the world thought those women were stunningly beautiful. Though makeup and camerawork could do amazing things for anyone, some of them really *were*.

But despite that, he couldn't remember the last time

he'd wanted to drag someone he'd just met to the nearest flat surface and make love to her in every way known to man. Until now.

Hot and damp with exertion, Bonnie swept her hair off the back of her neck with one hand. Holding it up, she looked so damned sultry, so feminine, every guy around paused to take a second look. She stole his breath, practically stopped his heart.

Drew stepped close. "You do know what you do to me, right?"

She blinked. "Excuse me?"

He let his stare answer, unable to look away from her full, pouty lips, her soft shoulders, and then at the green fabric molding the delicate curves of her body. The thin material did sinful things to the slopes of her breasts, outlining her pert nipples. No way was she wearing anything underneath, and he knew the brush of his lips there would feel *so* good—to both of them.

It had been a long time since he'd had his mouth on a woman. Too long. And he was suddenly starving, desperate for a taste.

"Stop," she ordered, her voice breathy and weak.

"Stop what?"

"Stop looking at me like…"

"Like I want you?"

She sucked in an audible breath. From a few inches away, he saw her pinken, as if all the blood in her body had gone to her skin to ready it for sensory input: his touch, his kiss, his tongue. He would be more than happy to give it to her. All that, and more.

"You can't," she whispered, dropping her hair.

"Can't want you, or can't have you?"

"Either. Both. I don't know."

"Which is it?"

She shook her head slowly. "Are you serious?"

"More serious than you can imagine."

"But I'm not…"

"Exactly," he said, knowing what she was going to say. "You're nothing like the women I know and work with."

"Right."

"Which, believe me, is a very good thing." Seeing her skepticism, he stepped closer. He slid one foot between hers, so their thighs tangled together as they moved to a slower, torchy song. Dropping one hand onto her hip, he stroked her lightly, wanting to fill both hands with those curves as he thrust into her.

"You are so far out of my league," she insisted, as if she really didn't know she was beyond beautiful and so sexy she would catch the attention of any man on earth.

"I can't help who I'm attracted to, Bonnie. Can you?"

She slowly shook her head, whispering, "No. And believe me, I've been trying."

"Why?" he asked, knowing instinctively what she meant. She'd been trying to hide her attraction to him.

"Because of who we are and where we are and how crazy the very idea of it is."

"Why is it crazy to want someone who you can't stop thinking about? Because I can't, you know. Can't stop thinking about you, picturing being with you." He intentionally brushed against her, knowing she had to feel the physical effect she had on him. She quivered in his arms and he whispered, "I want you, Bonnie. I want to make love to you."

She still hesitated, looking up at him with confusion, wonder. Snagging her bottom lip between her teeth, she was racked with indecision, he could see it in her eyes. She didn't know what to think; wasn't sure she could believe him. But chemistry didn't lie, and the desire between them was so thick he could bathe in it.

"If I can't have you, please say so. Otherwise I'm just going to keep thinking about it. If you're involved with someone else, or you don't feel the same way, tell me now."

"I'm not…" She half lowered her lashes. "…and I do."

He leaned in, breathing in the warm, spicy essence of her thick honey-gold hair. Catching a handful of it—soft, so incredibly soft—he held her tightly against his body, each of her curves softening in welcome to his angles. They lined up perfectly, top to bottom, as if they'd been made for each other. They just matched.

She shivered once, then softened, melted. Said yes, without saying a word.

"I know you came to my room thinking I was some big-bad-movie-star," he told her, wanting to get rid of any misconceptions before they took one more step.

"You are some big-bad-movie-star."

"Not bad," he promised. "At heart, I'm the guy who likes Disney movies and animals and would have cared about those little birds you were trying to protect last spring."

She tilted her head back and looked up at him. "Truly?"

"Yes. I'm just a small-town guy from Oregon who got really lucky and caught the eye of a director who was shooting a TV pilot in my hometown. I live in California now because I work there. But that *so* does not define who I really am."

He knew it sounded like a line, and wondered if she'd

believe it, but it was the truth. His address might have changed since he got his big break seven years ago. But he hadn't.

"No, you don't seem to be that type. Giving up your room, showing up here, putting up with this crowd… you really are a nice guy, aren't you?" She wasn't the first one to express surprise at that. It came with the territory.

"The friends I hang out with are old college buddies, not actors. And you don't see me in tabloids with actresses on my arms because the last time I dated one was in high school when I went out with the leading lady from *The Music Man.*"

"You're not involved with anyone now?"

"No. I was until about a year ago, but since we broke up, I haven't had time to even think of meeting anyone for a drink."

A tiny smile appeared. "You and I had a drink together."

He squeezed her. "Does that count as our first date, then?"

Laughing lightly, she said, "A date? Do movie stars date?"

"They do if they want to show a woman she means more than a notch on a headboard." He tightened his hold on her hips. "I'm not looking to notch my headboard. If I wanted that, I could nod at Miss French Maid or someone like her."

She moved her mouth close to his neck, so that her warm exhalations brushed his throat. Then even closer, until it was her soft lips he felt there. "What are you looking for?"

"I'm not sure. A night with you? Or a thousand nights

with you? Whatever we want to do together between those nights?"

Bonnie shuddered against him, so he could feel the V of her thighs against his leg. A warm, womanly scent of desire arose from her, and her eyes were suddenly smoky with wanting as she looked up at him. "I think that first night is pretty close. As close as the last room in the east wing of the inn."

His room. "You're sure?"

"Oh, yes. I've wanted you since I met you. I just didn't think there was any way you could feel the same way."

"I do," he insisted. "Can we get out of here, now?"

She nodded, and without another word, they stopped dancing and headed for the exit. Her fingers laced in his, they crossed the gauntlet of cooing females and moviegoing males.

"You're leaving?" asked Amanda, the bride, who had just said good-night to another departing guest.

"Yes," Drew said. "Bonnie's going to make sure I get to my door."

Bonnie smiled at her sister-in-law, her eyes shining brightly. "Yep, you can count on me to do my duty."

Saying good-night, they stepped outside. The very second the door slid closed behind them, Drew had her in his arms. She melted against him, lifting her mouth for his kiss, parting her lips invitingly. Their tongues met and danced a slow tango, deep and sultry, and he knew their first time would be just like that. Hot and deep and slow.

"I want you so badly I could take you right here against the building," he admitted as he ended the kiss and scraped his mouth along her jaw.

"Ditto," she said with a soft moan. "But I want a lot of

privacy because I have absolutely no intention of being quiet or *nice* tonight."

"Mmm. Sounds good. Am I going to meet the wicked Bonnie?"

She looked up at him, her eyes heavy-lidded with desire. "You might be the first person to know the *real* me, Drew. God knows I'm tired of hiding what I really feel, what I truly want."

He knew what she meant. She wanted *him*, just as he wanted her. "Let's go," he said, needing that privacy more and more.

But with the very first step they took out from under the protective covering of the barn awning, they were hit with a light, misty rain. Her thin dress was no match for it, and instantly began to stick to her skin. Which looked sexy as hell, but couldn't feel very comfortable.

"Uh-oh," she said, then glanced back into the party. "I left my umbrella hanging on the coatrack. I'll go..."

No way did he want her walking back in there for any other guy to see the way that damp green material clung to her breasts, outlining the most perfect nipples he'd ever seen. His mouth was already watering for a taste.

"Let me," he whispered, meaning a lot more than just going to get her umbrella. But that would do for a start.

"Sure you can be without your babysitter?"

"I'm a big boy."

The look she gave him was wicked...lascivious. As if she were really looking forward to finding out.

"Hold that thought," he ordered.

"Deal. The umbrella's bright red, you can't miss it."

Nodding, he headed back inside, hoping to escape unnoticed to the coatrack. He should have known better, however. Every two feet, somebody stopped him to tell him how much they liked his movies or ask what he was doing in town.

It was a good ten minutes before he got back outside, an apology on his lips. "I'm so sorry, I…"

His words trailed off when he realized he was talking to air. Bonnie wasn't there. He peered into the shadows on either side of the door, seeing nothing.

"Damn."

He just couldn't believe it. She'd changed her mind, gotten cold feet. Yeah, they were moving pretty fast, but she wanted him, he knew that. He just wouldn't ever have imagined she would leave without talking to him about it first.

Frustrated, wondering how he could get her room number at this time of night, he suddenly caught sight of something several feet way. A splash of color lay in some rocks that led down a garden pathway. The color was familiar, and he walked over, growing a bit more uneasy with every step he took. When he reached it, bent down and saw that it was, indeed, a piece of Bonnie's dress, his uneasiness grew to concern.

When he saw its jagged edge, proof that it had been torn, his concern grew to worry. But he didn't really panic until he saw what was lying beside it: a sexy, high-heeled shoe.

Maybe the dress could have caught on the bushes by accident, but no way did the woman go walking off into the night without a shoe.

Which, he feared, meant she hadn't *voluntarily* walked off at all. She'd been taken.

4

BONNIE COULDN'T BELIEVE IT. She'd been on the verge of going back to the room of the sexiest man she'd ever met in her life to have wild sex…and she got kidnapped. Well, not *technically* kidnapped—she hadn't been thrown into the trunk of a car and driven far away—but she was definitely being kept against her will. Talk about bad luck.

"Let me out!" she ordered, pounding her fist against the door, still shocked by what had just happened.

One minute, she'd been waiting for Drew to come back with her umbrella. The next, she'd heard a woman's voice calling for help from the side of the barn. Worrying some mildly intoxicated party guest had fallen and couldn't get up, she'd headed toward the woman, and found herself grabbed by a bushy-haired redhead who outweighed her by a good fifty pounds. The woman had stuck something against her back, told Bonnie she had a gun, then marched her down a hill, over a tiny footbridge and right into this storage shed. Where she'd promptly locked Bonnie in.

It could have been worse, she supposed. Her assailant could have actually used the gun—*if* she'd really had one.

Something told Bonnie there had been no gun, but she hadn't taken any chances. Especially not once she figured out she was dealing with Drew's stalker. Helen Jarvis had made it clear that the only person going back to Drew Ericson's room with him tonight would be her.

On reflection, though, Bonnie had to admit, the woman had been more pathetic than scary. Changing tactics, she said, "Miss Jarvis? Please, just let me out. You know you can't do this. You're going to get into even more trouble."

"You're a home-wrecker!" a muffled voice said from outside.

As a social worker for the city of Pittsburgh, Bonnie worked on a daily basis with people who had mental disorders. So she knew better than to try to challenge the woman's delusions directly. "Keeping someone against their will is against the law. You don't want to get in trouble with the police, do you?"

Silence for a moment. Then, "I'm not keeping you. Just hiding you for a little while."

Bonnie didn't have to ask why. The woman was "hiding" her so she could get Drew alone.

"Now you just stay quiet and somebody will find you in the morning," the woman said.

"The morning? No! You have to let me out now." Coughing, she added, "There are chemicals in here. They're making me sick."

That was a bit of an exaggeration, but she feared it wouldn't be for long. There were lawn chemicals in the shed. It was too dark to see much, but she could certainly smell them. Fertilizer, weed killer, insect repellant, probably all kinds of poisonous stuff that put off fumes. She wasn't sick yet, but she had no doubt she would be if she were stuck in here for hours.

"Hold your breath," the woman said.

"*All* night?"

"Well…I guess I could call and have someone come and let you out after Drew and I leave."

"Leave to go where?"

"Home, of course. To our place in California. We live in a mansion in Beverly Hills with lots of bedrooms for when we start a family."

Oh, boy. This woman was cuckoo for Cocoa Puffs. And while Bonnie still felt sorry for her, she was also really getting annoyed. The burning smell of some kind of chlorine-based chemical was seeping into her nose and she now could make out the scent of gasoline, too.

"Look, you and Drew can leave," she said, trying to play into the woman's fantasy. "I won't get in your way, just please let me out of here."

Her captor didn't answer right away. Bonnie held her breath, hopeful. So far, the woman seemed sadly delusional, but Helen Jarvis didn't act as though she truly wanted to hurt her.

Then the answer came…and her hopes were dashed.

"No. Now I'm going, just try to take a nap or something and someone will let you out soon."

Take a nap? Fall asleep while breathing in gasoline and all these other nasty fumes? Sure. Right. Only if she wanted to risk not waking up.

Now angry again, Bonnie pounded on the door and yelled. But this time, there was no answer, not even the slightest brush of a hand against the outside of the shed. She knew, deep down, that Helen Jarvis was gone, leaving Bonnie trapped.

And nobody knew where she was.

She didn't panic. There were a hundred people in the barn less than thirty yards away. Her entire family, her friends. Surely somebody would hear her if she kept yelling.

Over that music? And the chatter?

"Maybe not. But Drew will be looking."

Unless he decided you changed your mind and ditched him.

Frankly, if she had come back out and found him gone, that's exactly what she would have surmised.

Hell.

She might actually be stuck in here for a couple of hours—at least until the party ended and the noise died down enough for any stragglers to hear her. As soon as the music stopped, she'd start screaming.

But as the fumes grew stronger, and her head grew lighter, another worry blossomed. What if she passed out? If she lost consciousness before she had a chance to make herself heard, she could really be trapped in here overnight.

Leaning toward the seam between door and jamb, she sucked in a breath, grateful for the hint of cool moisture from the fresh air she managed to inhale. Feeling her way along the seam, she found a wider spot farther down, at about knee level. Sinking to the floor, she focused on breathing through that opening, keeping her forehead resting against the door. Her heart was thudding now, her imagination taking her places she didn't want to go.

What if Helen forgot where she'd left her? What if

she ran from the police and never got a chance to tell anyone what she'd done? Or, what if she didn't get what she wanted from Drew—as she certainly would not— and was so angry, she intentionally let Bonnie rot? It was after midnight, on Sunday. The groundskeepers almost certainly would not be working in the morning, especially in this weather. So might she be stuck in here until Monday?

Her eyes had grown slightly accustomed to the shadowy darkness, and she looked around the small, ten-by-ten-foot structure. As she had suspected, bags of dried chemicals were stacked all around her; large containers of liquids with Poison markings, too.

"You can't stay here until Monday," she whispered, reaching for the door handle, jiggling it again, though she knew it was useless. As far as she could tell, Helen Jarvis had apparently put some kind of padlock on the outside. No way was she getting out of here without help.

They'll come looking. In the morning, when she didn't show up for the bridal breakfast, somebody would come looking for her, realize her bed hadn't been slept in and would start a search. So at the very worst, she just had to hold out until 9:00 or 10:00 a.m. Eight hours, tops. "You can do that."

Especially if she had no other choice.

Time seemed to be passing—the music played on— but Bonnie wasn't sure if it had been twenty minutes or an hour. She only knew that each breath she inhaled was a little more labored than the last. Her throat was hurting now, her nose burning, her eyes watering.

"Please," she whispered, "please find me."

She didn't add a name to the plea, but deep down,

she knew who she was talking to. He played a hero in his movies. Now she needed Drew Ericson to be one in real life.

"YOU'RE TELLING ME BONNIE was grabbed by some crazy, jealous stalker?" Reese Campbell asked, glowering at Drew.

"I don't know," he said, remaining calm, not giving in to the deep worry that had gripped him from the minute he found Bonnie's shoe. "But can you see your sister just kicking off one of her high heels and traipsing away?"

"No," Reese said.

His wife, Amanda, who had walked outside for some fresh air a minute or two after Drew had found the shoe—then gone in and quietly gotten her husband—jumped in. "We'll call the police. Get everyone at the party to start searching."

Drew thought about it. "Listen, if it is Helen Jarvis, getting a hundred people out here hunting for her could make things worse. If she's panicked, and cornered, she…"

"Might hurt Bonnie?" Reese asked, his jaw rigid.

"She has no record of violence," Drew insisted, trying to keep himself calm. "But there's no point in putting her into a frenzy until we have to. You call the police, I'll call the head of security from the studio—they have pictures of her. Then you and I will start searching until they get here. Maybe we can find Bonnie without setting the woman off."

"All right," Reese said, reaching for his cell phone. "We'll do it your way. For now."

"Yes, we *all* will," said Amanda, glaring at her husband. "I'm searching, too."

Her husband pointed to her costume—a long, ragged

gown. Drew wasn't sure what she was supposed to be. "In that?"

"Just let me run to my room and change." She didn't even wait for him to answer before darting toward the inn, never looking back.

"Check Bonnie's room, just to be sure," Reese called after her.

"Already planning to," she replied, not slowing down.

"I'm sorry as hell about this," Drew said. "I should never have left her alone to go after that damned umbrella."

Reese nodded once, then turned his attention to his phone, talking to the police. Drew took the time to make his own call to the production assistant who'd phoned earlier. Telling him to get security out here, pronto, he then hung up.

"Okay, why don't we split up. You search from here to the west side of the lawn, toward the inn. I'll go to the other side, down toward the road," Drew said. Bending down, he picked up a brown paper bag, weighted with sand. Inside was a battery-operated electric candle, which, when removed from the luminary, produced a decent amount of light.

"Good idea," Reese said, doing the same thing. "Let's meet back here in ten minutes."

"Okay."

Without another word, Drew headed toward the road, skirting the barn. He passed the spot where he'd found Bonnie's shoe, and that ripped scrap of fabric. The grass was damp and slippery beneath his shoes and he half skidded down the slope. Today's rain had lifted the small, gurgling creek and it gushed powerfully beneath the pretty footbridge.

Reaching the wooden crossing, he spotted something, squatted down and shone the candle on the spot.

Footprints. One of which was bare.

His heart racing, he ran across the bridge, scanning wildly for anyplace she could be. None of the guest cabins were on this side of the property, just a few out-buildings, then a stand of woods separating the lawn from the road. He only hoped Helen Jarvis hadn't had a car waiting. If she'd whisked Bonnie off the property, God only knew where she was by now.

Refusing to think that way, he decided to call out, hoping if she was nearby, she'd be able to hear him. "Bonnie? Do you hear me?"

He heard nothing at first, nothing but the gurgle of the creek and the deejay working the party.

"Bonnie?"

A noise. Something thumped. He swung his head around, spying a maintenance shed not twenty feet away. Striding toward it, he hadn't taken more than a few steps when he heard her voice.

"Please help me—is somebody out there?"

"Bonnie!"

He charged to the door, seeing a padlock hooked through the latch. But Helen Jarvis had either been in a hurry, or she'd had some attack of conscience, because the lock wasn't snapped shut. It had kept Bonnie from getting out, but didn't prevent him from opening the door from the outside. As soon as he did, he saw a form crumpled on the floor. "Oh, God, Bonnie!"

"Drew?" she asked, turning her dirty, pale face up to him.

Drew dropped to his knees and pulled her into his arms. "It's okay, I've got you," he said, holding her tight, saying a little mental prayer of thanks that she didn't seem hurt.

Her face was buried in his neck, but he felt the sting of moisture from recently shed tears. She coughed weakly, her chest rattling. The air in the shed reeked of chemicals. His eyes stung after mere seconds, and she'd been trapped for almost an hour.

"We've got to get you outside," he said, rising to his feet, lifting her as he went. Holding her tightly in his arms, he stepped back out into the clear night.

She sucked in a few deep, grateful breaths. Keeping her arms curled around his neck, she stayed cuddled against him, as if not wanting to let go. Which was just fine. He had no intention of putting her down anytime soon. He wanted to keep her right where she was, safe in his embrace.

Though he needed to get her back up the hill so her brother would know she was all right, Drew gave her a minute to even out her breathing. Pressing soft kisses onto her temple, he whispered, "You're okay, it's over," again and again.

Finally she took a last deep, cleansing breath, then murmured, "How did you find me?"

"I saw your shoe on the ground, and a piece of your dress."

A pout tugged at her beautiful lips. "She made me rip my dress? I worked so hard on it."

"I know you did, sweetheart, and I'm so sorry." Already fairly certain he knew the answer, he asked, "Who took you? Was it a middle-aged woman with red hair?"

Bonnie nodded. "She told me she was Helen Jarvis. She saw me as some kind of floozy trying to steal 'her' man and was trying to get me out of the way."

His whole body tensed, his teeth clenching so hard he was surprised they didn't crack. "This has gone far enough!"

She ran the tips of her fingers up the tight cords of muscle in his neck. "I'm okay. She didn't hurt me and said she'd send someone back to find me."

He wasn't mollified. "Before or after you choked on fumes?"

Sighing, she admitted, "Yeah, that had me worried, too."

He squeezed her a little tighter. "I'm so sorry, Bonnie. Please forgive me. I can't believe you were exposed to that kind of danger because of me."

She shook her head. "I wasn't exposed to that kind of danger because of you—it was all because a mentally unstable woman took me. It is *not* your fault."

Maybe, but she wouldn't have drawn the attention of Helen Jarvis if it weren't for him. He'd brought one of the darkest parts of his crazy, frenetic world into the bright, happy sphere of this woman's, and couldn't feel much worse about that if he'd hurt her himself. "Thanks," he muttered. "But I think we both know my line of work invites this kind of bullshit. I should never have…"

She stared into his eyes. "Should never have what? Invited me to your room? Told me you wanted me?"

He didn't answer. Because, though that's what he meant, he just couldn't say it out loud. Deep down, he couldn't regret trying to make something happen with Bonnie. After just one kiss, he already knew she was someone special. Someone he wanted to spend a lot more time with. *One night? A thousand nights?*

"Don't you back out on me now, hotshot," she ordered. "If you think this gets you off the hook and you don't have to give me tonight or a thousand nights and everything that comes between them, you've got another think coming."

Smiling faintly as she echoed his thoughts, and his earlier words, he said, "Are you sure about that?"

She lifted her face, until her lips were a scant inch from his own, her sweet breath brushing his face, the warm scent of her perfume filling the night air, chasing away any remnants of the fumes. "I'm very sure," she whispered.

Then Bonnie removed that inch of space, brushing her mouth gently against his in a kiss that was as sweet as their first one had been passionate. Her mouth was soft and yielding. Tender.

He'd kissed many women in movies, and more than a few in real life. But he'd never quite gotten just how thrilling a simple kiss could be, until it was Bonnie Campbell's mouth, her hands around his neck, her breaths he shared, her soft hair brushing his face, her beautiful body enfolded in his arms.

Moaning a little, she tilted her head, parting her lips. Their tongues slid together in a soft exploration, slow and lazy. Against him, her heart pounded. His own sped up its pace, too. The beats seemed to find one another, to come together in unison as one hard, demanding thud.

But they were outside, and that misty rain was beginning to fall again. Her brother was worried sick about her. And a crazy woman who'd kidnapped her could still be lurking nearby. So, filled with regret, he ended the kiss.

Bonnie smiled lazily. "I liked that."

"Me, too."

"I want a lot more of those."

"Tonight?" he asked, making absolutely sure she hadn't had a change of heart.

"For a start."

Yeah. For a start. That sounded just fine to him.

As the rain started falling a little harder, Drew turned and walked back toward the footbridge. He trod carefully over it, and just as carefully up the hill, holding her still. She insisted she was okay and that he could put her down, but frankly, he wasn't ready to let her out of his arms.

Once they got back to the barn, he immediately looked for her brother, but didn't see him. He did, however, see the distinctive blue twirl of police lights up by the inn, as well as a number of people outside talking.

Heading that way, he let Bonnie down when Reese and Amanda appeared from within the crowd, spotted them and hurried over.

"Bonnie! Are you okay?" Reese asked, grabbing her and pulling her in for a tight hug.

"I'm fine. Just got locked in a storage shed."

Drew noticed she downplayed the incident, not wanting her brother to know just how dangerous the situation could have become had she been left there much longer.

"Well, it's over now, you're safe," said Amanda. "And that crazy woman is never going to bother you again."

Drew turned his attention to the bride, hearing a note of certainty in her voice. "They caught her?"

Amanda snagged her bottom lip between her teeth, slowly shaking her head. "Not exactly."

Reese, who had let Bonnie go, dropped an arm across his wife's shoulders. "Manda did."

Bonnie gasped and Drew raised a shocked brow.

"Apparently your admirer didn't do her research. She didn't know you'd moved out of the bridal suite," Amanda explained.

Drew, remembering that Amanda had been going back to the room to change, immediately understood. "Did she hurt you?"

Reese barked a laugh. "Uh, that'd be the other way around."

Amanda smirked. "And you thought I didn't need to take those kickboxing classes."

"Just remind me to never grab for you in the dark," Reese said. Then, with a "duh" look on his face, said, "Wait. Scratch that. What the hell am I thinking? It is our wedding night."

"One of the most exciting on record," she said with a laugh.

Turning to Bonnie and Drew, Reese explained, "The woman jumped out at her and my blushing bride starting swinging."

"It was purely reflex," Amanda said, sounding sheepish about having brawled on her wedding night. "She surprised me."

"Well, it should be no surprise to anyone that she's handcuffed in the back of a police car." His laughter fading, Reese sounded much more serious as he said, "She's facing charges for a lot more than stalking now. Kidnapping, assault and breaking and entering, to start with."

Good. If there was any justice in the world, the woman would be forced to get treatment for her mental issues. And if she didn't, prison was no more than she deserved for what could have happened to Bonnie if she'd been left to breathe in those chemicals all night long.

"The police are going to want to interview you, Bonnie," Amanda said. "We should let them know you're okay."

Bonnie nodded. "I am. Thanks to Drew." She smiled up at him. "I guess you really are a hero."

"Hardly."

"Well, you are in my book," she insisted. Then she rose on tiptoe and brushed a kiss across his cheek. Whispering so she wouldn't be overheard by her brother and his wife, she added, "And I'm looking forward to giving you a hero's welcome just as soon as I'm finished with the police."

5

BONNIE SPENT A HALF HOUR talking to the police before they left, taking a crying Helen Jarvis with them. Despite what she'd done, Bonnie felt a little sorry for the woman, who obviously had the faculties to realize she was in serious trouble. In fact, as soon as she'd been told she was being arrested, she'd started apologizing, saying she knew she'd crossed the line, she just wanted Drew so much she didn't know what else to do. She knew right from wrong, knew she had no real relationship with Drew.

Which, as a slightly more jaded Amanda pointed out, had probably shot any insanity defense.

It was well after 2:00 a.m. by the time they said their good-nights. They'd tried to leave earlier, but every time another person came back to the inn from the party down at the barn, the story had to be repeated and retold, and Bonnie had to assure yet another friend or family member that she was just fine.

Oh, and Drew had to stand there and be cooed and gushed over and called a hero again.

Finally, though, they managed to slip away. Fortunately Bonnie's room was just down the hall from Drew's, so she didn't think they raised too many eyebrows by walking off together. Frankly, though, even if they had, she didn't care. She'd been waiting for this—waiting to kiss him again, touch him, feel him, for hours.

They went by unspoken agreement to his room. Unlocking the door, he gestured for her to go in, then followed.

Alone with him at last, Bonnie waited for something—a flash of unease, of embarrassment, of awkwardness. But there was nothing. Just certainty of what she was doing, what she wanted. And him, watching her from a few feet away, staring at her like he wanted to memorize her every feature.

"You sure you're okay?" he asked. "Your throat's not sore?"

"I'm fine," she assured him.

Bonnie fell silent as he came closer, his body radiating warmth. When he was just a few inches away, she swayed toward him, drawn by his heat, his smell and the hunger in those clear blue eyes.

He smiled slowly in the semidarkness. "You take my breath away."

Before she realized his intention, he'd caught her in his arms, drawing her against his body. She wrapped her arms around his waist and tilted her head back, silently urging him to close that final few inch gap and kiss her.

She didn't have long to wait. In a moment shorter than a heartbeat his lips were on hers, and she sighed. His kiss was all she remembered, and all she imagined. Deep and wet and powerful. He slid the palms of his hands up and down on her back, then around to cup her arms, then finally down to wrap his fingers in hers.

"I am so glad I met you, Drew," she whispered as he

moved his lips to kiss her jaw. "Really met you this time, rather than just crossing paths, like we did six months ago."

"If we had really met six months ago," he told her, "we'd already have a hundred and eighty nights like this behind us."

He sounded so sure of it, as if he already knew this—tonight—wasn't possibly going to be enough for either of them. "I'd know exactly how to touch you," he whispered, kissing her earlobe, then her nape. "Where to kiss you, when to go slow and when to go wild."

Bonnie groaned, his words turning her on as much as his touch. "You're a fast learner," she told him, almost whimpering as he scraped the palm of his hand all the way down her arm, stroking so lightly she almost couldn't feel the connection of skin on skin. The barely there caress built her anticipation, leaving her wondering where he would touch next. Where that hand would go, which part of her body he'd kiss or taste.

Bonnie's breath came faster as Drew moved his fingers to her neck and gently began stroking the tender skin beneath her ear. Slowly, so slowly it nearly drove her insane, he trailed the tips of his fingers across her collarbone, then down to the deep V in the front of her dress. Pressing his mouth to her nape, he deftly tugged one sleeve down off her shoulder.

"Mmm," she moaned, wanting more. So much more. His fingers slipped down over the curve of her breast, teasing, tempting. She arched toward him. "Yes, there."

"We've got plenty of time."

She saw his smile just before he captured her mouth in another kiss. She shivered, from the pleasure, from the relief of giving in to arousal that had pounded inside her all evening. From pure, utter want.

"I want you more than I've ever wanting anything," he whispered against her lips as he drew her tighter in his arms.

Bonnie didn't say a word as he lifted her hands up to his mouth and pressed kisses on her fingers, slowly, with the patience of Job. She had the feeling he would be just this slow, just this deliberate, with every single step tonight. Every kiss would be a celebration, each stroke an exploration.

She could hardly wait.

"Are you cold?" he asked.

The room *was* cool with the October night air, but Bonnie didn't think she'd ever felt more hot. Her clothes stuck to her, annoying her sensitive flesh, and she nearly purred as Drew slid her dress from her other shoulder, pushing it to the floor until she stood there, wearing nothing but a tiny pair of panties.

"I'm just fine," she finally said, in answer to his question.

"You're much more than fine," he whispered as he looked down at her.

Bonnie felt no embarrassment as his eyes traveled over her body. The pure appreciation—the desire—was enough to give her a great deal of confidence. She saw the pulse in his temple pound and watched him part his lips and draw in a deep breath. Her skin tingled in reaction and she felt her nipples grow even harder under his gaze. As if he couldn't resist, he bent and pressed his mouth to the top curve of her breast.

"More," she begged.

He took his time, slowly kissing his way down her breast to the hard, sensitive tip. Even then, he didn't suckle her right away, as she wanted. Instead he brushed his lips across her, back and forth, so patient, so deliberate.

"Please!"

Only when she revealed her desperation did he comply, covering her nipple with his mouth and sucking deeply.

"God, yes," she groaned, twining her hands in his thick, black hair. She moaned. Her knees weakened.

Realizing it, Drew slid an arm around her waist, holding her up, fully supporting her weight. She was helpless to resist as he paid careful attention to both breasts. And she didn't even try to refuse when he lifted her into his arms and carried her over to the turned-down bed.

Placing her down upon it, Drew stood beside her and began to strip out of his clothes. When he lifted his shirt over his head and tossed it away, she hissed. She hadn't imagined it—the man did have the most perfect male body she had ever seen.

"You really shouldn't answer the door to your hotel room dressed only in a towel," she said with a throaty, hungry chuckle. "You have no idea of your effect on women. It can give them the wildest ideas."

"I like your wild ideas," he told her.

His smile gleamed in the near-darkness as he finished stripping off his clothes. For a moment, she simply had to stare at him, a gasp catching in the back of her throat at that proud, hard shaft rising from between his legs.

It had been a long time since she'd been with a man. And she'd never been with a man built like *him*. Yet she didn't feel the slightest tinge of worry. Instead she was flooded with a fresh river of lust.

They'd fit. Oh, yes, they would fit.

Before tossing his pants aside, Drew reached into the

pocket and drew out a condom. She didn't ask where he got it, just glad he had it. "Come here," she ordered.

He knelt on the bed, letting her reach up, put her arms around his neck and draw him down toward her. She couldn't stop touching him, running her hands across all that slick male skin. It amazed her that his flesh could feel so warm and pliant, yet cover the hard, rippling muscles of a perfectly toned male body. Her fingertips felt electrified, and her excitement grew until she could hear nothing but the pounding of her own heart pumping hot blood through her veins.

Restless, she shifted her legs, wrapping them around his strong, heavier one, tugging him close. Through the thin film of her panties she felt his thick erection, and her body's own rush of answering moisture.

Drew reached for the tiny swatch of fabric and began to tug it down her legs, his touch burning a path on her skin. Then he moved his hand back up, reaching for the tuft of curls over her sex. Sliding one finger between the folds of her body, he groaned, as if driven a little more crazy to find her so wet, so hot, so ready. His thumb dropped onto her clit and he toyed with it, even as he slid one finger into her.

"More," she ordered. "Please, Drew, I want you inside me. Make love to me."

"Gladly."

After donning the condom, he moved over her, and she parted her legs in welcome. She wrapped her arms around his neck, drawing him down for a deep, wet kiss. As he began to ease into her, Bonnie arched up, greedy for more, wondering how the man was capable of such restraint. But he seemed determined to keep it slow, to draw out every sensation, every emotion. She was almost sobbing both with how good it felt, and how desperate she was for even more.

"Please," she whispered.

And finally, he complied, driving in all the way, deep and hard. There was no pain, she was completely ready for him, her softness yielding instantly to him. Bonnie believed she'd never felt anything more delicious in her life. She closed her eyes, determined to savor every deep sensation. She loved the heaviness of his body on hers, the roughness of his hair on her skin, the smell of his sweat, and the steady strokes which filled her.

There were no more words as the rhythm caught them and Bonnie gave herself over to it. Lost in sensation, she couldn't form another coherent thought as he filled her again and again until she cried out in delight, and he answered with a final powerful thrust and a groan.

Afterward, she lay beside him, both of them gasping for breath. Her heart was pounding like crazy, as if she'd run a marathon. She knew it was more than the physical exertion. Emotionally, she'd had a complete workout.

Drew kept an arm across her, holding her tightly against his body, as if loath to let her go. Finally their breathing slowed, the heart rates calmed, stillness descended. But he didn't seem finished. He kept touching her, caressing her, keeping her senses on alert, the waves of pleasure threatening to roll over her again.

Drew Ericson was the kind of lover women dreamed of, but seldom ever had. He was totally and completely attentive, thoroughly in the moment, utterly in tune with his senses and her own responses. Honestly, she didn't know if she would ever get enough of him. Considering she liked him so much already, admired him, enjoyed being with him and now was rapidly growing addicted to his lovemaking, she greatly feared he was going to be one habit that would be very hard to break.

As if he'd read her thoughts, and was thinking the same thing, Drew mused, "One night? Or a thousand nights?"

"I don't know," she replied. "What do you think?"

He moved his mouth to hers, kissing her sweetly, softly, so tender and erotic at the same time. When he looked at her, his blue eyes gleamed. He made no effort to hide the raw emotion.

"What I think, in my gut, my intuition and in the very bottom of my heart, Bonnie Campbell, is that *ten thousand* nights is never going to be enough for us." He moved his mouth toward hers, and just before covering it in a kiss, added, "But it'll do for a start."

* * * * *

Halfway There

1

SERVING AS HER BEST friend Amanda's maid of honor,
Jocelyn—Jazz—Wilkes knew exactly what her job
entailed.

She was in charge of stuff like making sure the bride's
veil was straight, or holding her dress up and out of the
way if she had to pee. She'd straightened Amanda's train,
held the bouquet during the exchange of rings, handed
the bride a tissue when she started to cry during the
groom's heartfelt recitation of the vows.

She'd seen to it that the flower girl didn't pick her
nose throughout the ceremony, and, of course, she had
a getaway car parked out back in case the bride got cold
feet at the last minute—which, knowing how madly in
love Amanda was with her groom, she doubted. In general, she'd been responsible for handling all the gal-pal
stuff only the best of friends could ever depend on each
other for.

She'd taken this maid of honor stuff seriously from
day one. There wasn't a ribbon she hadn't tied, or a
shower invitation she hadn't written or a dress fitting
she hadn't attended.

Never having failed at anything—and loving

Amanda like the sister she'd never had—Jazz had been
determined to do the job right. She'd been Thelma to
Amanda's Louise for years, the two of them having become best friends when they'd realized they were so
much alike—two strong females working in a male
dominated industry. There was nothing she wouldn't
do for the other woman.

Which was why she now dutifully stood with all the
other horny single females, watching as the bouquet
came sailing out of Amanda's hands, over her head, to
the crowd waiting at the base of the staircase. Though
Jazz was completely apathetic about it, maids of honor
were all about tradition, and Jazz was gonna go down
in history as the kick-assingest maid of honor ever.

"Outta my way, ladies!"

"It's mine!"

Ignoring the other women leaping into the air like
brightly colored jack-in-the-boxes, Jazz remained quietly
in her little section of floor space. She didn't lunge for
the bouquet, didn't elbow anybody or do her impersonation of roller derby princess to get at it. Nor, however,
did she leap out of the line of fire to avoid it.

She was there, a part of things, even if, frankly, in
her opinion, the whole bouquet-toss was a silly tradition. She couldn't care less whether she caught the thing
or not. She just had to do her bit and collect her green
Participant ribbon.

It appeared right away that the green ribbon was the
only one she'd be getting in this particular contest. The
blue one appeared to be heading toward Abby, Amanda's
sister, who, though she'd once seemed to have a major
stick up her ass, was actually a pretty decent chick. She
hadn't been at all bitchy about not having been chosen
as maid of honor, despite being Amanda's only sibling.

And she'd done a great job as wedding planner. She'd even been a lot of fun at Manda's bachelorette party, letting down her hair and dancing her butt off with the rest of them.

Right now, though, Abby didn't look happy. In fact, as the bouquet came barreling toward her face, she looked like someone about to be swarmed by bees. That *hell-no* expression gave a one-second warning to her next move, so it really came as no surprise when Abby swung at the bouquet, flinging it away from herself like it was contaminated with cooties.

Interesting. Especially since she was engaged to be married to a hunk of stiff lawyer who stood watching the event from a few yards away.

Jazz glanced over at said lawyer, saw the shock—maybe even a flash of hurt—in his face, and realized Abby was gonna have some 'splaining to do. Considering both sets of parents were glowering, it would be a lot of 'splaining. Jazz was very happy not to be in that woman's shoes at the moment.

"Okay, everyone, let's make way for the guys to try for the garter!" someone called.

Checking the "stand there and pretend you give a crap about a bunch of flowers" thing off her mental list, Jazz drifted toward the ballroom, where the reception had been held. She intended to make a beeline for the open bar. Having laid off the alcohol today, wanting to be sharp and *on* for all her jazzy M.O.H. duties, she felt entitled to a little R & R—or Jack and Coke—now that the reception was winding down.

While the women squeezed away to make room for the men, who were sucked into the open space like dust bunnies into a vacuum, she again took stock of all the single guys present. She'd been on the lookout since last night, at the rehearsal, for an appropriate wedding flirtation candidate, but still hadn't found anyone who caught her interest.

As maid of honor, she would normally have first looked to the best man, but considering he was Reese's teenage brother, that was a no-go. But the other groomsmen were all single, as far as she knew. And there were lots of Campbell cousins and guys who worked for Reese at the brewery, not to mention some sexy young things from the airport where she and Amanda worked.

Funny thing was, none of them really rang her bell. The very cocky groomsman, Tom, who Amanda had warned her about, looked like a gigolo and would probably have to be handled with venereal-disease-proof kid gloves. One of the other ushers was already drunk and sloppy, another appeared totally infatuated with one of Reese's many sisters. The guys from the airport were too familiar, the ones from the brewery too cozy with the Campbell family to hit up the bride's best friend.

There was, of course, one other option.

Nope. Not going there. Don't even think about it.

No, she couldn't let her thoughts go in that direction, wouldn't allow herself to consider *him*. Blake Marshall.

The fact that the man had been on her mind so much was *completely* incidental. Because he was not her type. The two of them had about as much chance of hooking up as a stallion did with a beaver. *Don't think stallions and beavers. Especially not when you're thinking about him.*

She took in a deep, cleansing breath, acknowledging for the thousandth time that there was no way she was going to make a play for a guy who couldn't stand her.

Not even one she'd been having the most intense dreams about.

Not just sex dreams, either. Lately she'd been having strange, unusually sweet, romantic dreams about him, too.

Stop! If anything, those dreams just emphasized how wrong he was for her. Because romance hadn't been part of her repertoire for a long time. Not since she'd had her heart crushed under the heels of a couple of really heartless men.

"Hello, Jocelyn."

Closing her eyes briefly, she cringed, not even having to turn around to see who had spoken. She knew that voice. Knew that snobby tone. Knew the only person who refused to call her by her nickname. Knew that I'm-such-a-gentleman-nothing-you-can-do-will-ever-upset-me attitude.

It was her nemesis, the bane of her daily existence at O'Hare. The guy who could make her feel like something that had crawled out of the bottom of a garbage pit with one single, disapproving look. The guy she loved to hate and lived to shock. The one who was *so* not her type.

And who she couldn't stop thinking about. Fantasizing about. Dreaming about.

"Blake Marshall," she drawled, slowly turning around, forcing a casual smile to her face. "Fancy seeing you here."

Of course, she'd already seen him—he'd been around all day. Her stupid subconscious had probably made her walk in this direction.

"Nice wedding," he said.

"Very."

Inane, but about as much as she could manage right

now, until she figured out what else to say to Mr. Blake Marshall.

For some reason, Amanda had always really liked the guy. Jazz's first opinion of him, on the other hand, had been that he was a major pain in the ass. A drop-dead gorgeous one, yes, she'd always conceded that. But beyond his striking, boy-next-door good looks, she hadn't figured the man had much else to offer.

He was a customer relations manager, for heaven's sake, a yes-man who kissed corporate ass at the airport all day, calming angry passengers and smoothing over P.R. nightmares. He excelled at making nice and was so damned proper all the time, she'd sometimes been tempted to flash him just to see if he'd at least take a second look.

Only, lately, she was having a hard time remembering what she didn't like about him. And she was finding it much too easy to think about what she did.

"No luck with the bouquet, I see," he murmured, obviously having noticed that she'd participated in the so-not-Jazz-like event.

"Nope." Some wicked streak that always made her try to shock him had her adding, "Guess I'm just destined to sleep around rather than ever getting married."

"How fortunate for all the men in Chicago."

He said it so nicely, so evenly, she couldn't quite decide whether he was merely making conversation or had just totally insulted her. There was a hint of a smile on those really nice male lips, but whether it was because he almost always smiled or had just backhandedly called her a slut was anyone's guess.

"Why aren't you out there with all the other nerds trying to get a chance to cop a free feel on the blonde who caught the bouquet?"

Staring down at her, his handsome face absolutely expressionless, he replied, "I'm afraid she's not my type."

"Oh, 'cause she's female?"

Nothing. Not even the slightest flinch. The guy was uninsultable. Damn, that drove her nuts.

And, damn, why couldn't she bite her tongue? She just didn't seem to have a single bit of self-control around this man.

"She's a little too…blonde for my tastes."

She thought his gaze might have shifted to her own short, jet-black hair, but figured she had imagined it. Blake Marshall didn't like one single thing about her, she knew that much. Maybe that was why she always tried to get under his skin.

Blake Marshall. Even his name drove her nuts. It was a soap opera character name for God's sake. Just because he had the looks to match didn't make it any more acceptable. How could any guy be so damned perfect?

"Amanda and Reese seem like a great couple," he said, glancing out toward the stairway, where Reese was doing a sexy job of removing the garter from Manda's thigh.

"They are," she admitted with a faint smile. "Reese is a good guy. I think he might actually deserve her."

"I don't know him well, but he seems to make her happy."

"They're crazy about each other."

"I can tell."

Strange. She was having something resembling a normal conversation with Blake Marshall and wasn't yet tempted to do something totally inappropriate, if only to shock the man.

This simply wouldn't do.

"Are you enjoying yourself?" he asked, so polite, so proper, so frigging respectable.

"I was, but I'm not right at the moment," she admitted. Then, unable to help herself, added, "I can't seem to find the right lay for tonight."

His pleasant smile might have tightened the tiniest bit, the green eyes may have narrowed a smidge. Beyond that, nada. "Well, good luck with that."

"Thanks." Finally feeling like she'd made a teensy, weensy dent in his untarnished armor, she said, "Got any suggestions?"

"For?"

"For the traditional post-wedding hookup."

"Oh, is that a tradition, along with throwing birdseed and tying cans to the back of the groom's bumper?"

She shrugged. "It is in my book."

"Your book, huh?"

"What, you think just because I sling a hammer, I can't read?"

"No. I just think you're getting your books from the wrong library."

He sounded serious, not cool and snobby, as he usually did. That gave her pause for a second, and she had to wonder why he seemed to give a damn about anything she did, considering he didn't like her.

Then again, it was the wedding day of a mutual friend. If they couldn't call a truce today, they didn't deserve to be here.

"Want a drink? I was just about to have one to celebrate reaching the end of my maid of honor duties without any major incidents."

One brow lifted over a dark green eye, as if he didn't entirely trust her motives. Well, he did have reason. She had gone out of her way to annoy him whenever possible during the three years they'd worked together at the airport.

Amanda had once accused her of being Lucy to Blake's Charlie Brown. Like she delighted in antagonizing him because she secretly had a crush on the man.

Jazz had snorted with laughter at the time. Now, though? Well, she wasn't laughing anymore.

"Come on, let's call a truce today," she urged. "For Amanda's sake."

"A truce? I wasn't aware we were at war."

She snorted. "Gimme a break, you hate my guts."

That was the first thing she'd said that truly seemed to take him by surprise. His mouth fell open for a quick, shocked moment. Then he snapped it shut, slowly shaking his head. "You're wrong. You couldn't possibly be more wrong."

Jazz hesitated, hearing a note of sincerity there that genuinely surprised her. She'd been so sure this man couldn't stand her, yet his tone and his words said otherwise.

Maybe she'd been transferring her own feelings onto him.

Liar.

She had to concede, that wasn't it. She didn't hate Blake Marshall, not at all. He drove her absolutely crazy and managed to make her feel small with a single look, but she couldn't even pretend to dislike him anymore. In fact, she greatly feared Amanda was right. She did like him a little too much. On one particular occasion, she'd found him to be the most warm, sympathetic person she knew.

It had been at the airport several months ago. She'd been working late, alone in the hangar, and had looked up to see Blake there, watching her. He'd had such a look of sympathy and concern on his face, she'd immediately known something was wrong.

He'd told her the truth—one of her brothers, Danny, a Navy pilot stationed in the Middle East, was missing. Her own family didn't even know yet. The media had gotten wind of the story and contacted the airport, since Danny had worked for one of the major airlines before deciding to return to active duty.

Jazz's world had frozen in that moment. She knew she had to get to her parents' place, to stop her family from finding out from a stranger, yet she'd felt incapable of movement.

Blake had been right there, taking her in his arms, letting her sob and be weak and terrified for a few minutes. He'd said all the right things, given her strength and hope, then had insisted on driving her home.

Danny had ended up being fine. But on that night, when she'd been afraid she'd lost someone she dearly loved, Blake Marshall had been the one to hold her and keep the terror at bay. She'd allowed herself to forget how that had felt, how *he* had felt, holding her so tightly in his arms.

Now she remembered.

So, no. She didn't hate him. They might have gone back to their snarky relationship, but deep down, she'd known from that night on that he was one of the good guys. Even if he still drove her nuts.

Come on, you know it's more than that.

Maybe. It was at least possible that she found him attractive, but that didn't mean she would do anything about it. Because she knew he couldn't stand her.

Yet today, she found herself wanting to let down her

guard a little, relax and see if she could rediscover the man who'd held her in a rare moment of weakness. The man whose shoulders had been so incredibly broad, whose arms had been so very strong.

The man she liked. The man she dreamed of.

Licking her lips, she cast a quick, surreptitious look over his suit-clad form, noting again that the guy might have the mind of an executive, but he had the body of a porn star. All lean hips and broad chest and long legs. Yum.

What are you thinking? This is Blake Marshall!

Right. Blake Marshall. A man so totally unlike her, so out of her league that she'd never once considered trying to make a move on him, at least not when she was awake.

Why her thoughts were going that way now, she honestly couldn't say. She just knew that, suddenly— maybe because of the intense, vibrant way he'd said those words, *You couldn't possibly be more wrong,* she wanted to spend a little more time with the man. One-on-one time.

Naked one-on-one time.

If she'd already had a drink, she might have wondered if she was drunk even to think such a thing was really possible. But she was stone-cold sober. And *very* curious.

"So, if we're not at war, shall we just have a drink and toast to Amanda and Reese's happiness?" she asked, smiling brightly, hoping he didn't see how badly she wanted him to say yes.

He hesitated, staring at her for a long moment, then finally nodded. "All right then. One drink. For Amanda and Reese."

BLAKE DIDN'T WANT TO HAVE a drink with Jazz. He
didn't want to talk to Jazz. Didn't want to look at Jazz.
Didn't want to be anywhere near Jazz.

Because the closer to her he got, the closer he *wanted*
to get. And that was completely out of the question.

Desiring someone like Jazz Wilkes was like desiring
the worst, most painful, hug-the-toilet hangover of his
life. One incredible night of wild, crazy, addictive sex
followed by a day-after of sheer hell. Because he had no
doubt that's what would happen.

It wasn't that he hadn't been tempted to just go for
it. He had been, for a very long time. But he still had
some sense of self-preservation left, despite the way she
zapped his brain cells whenever she was in the same
room.

Jazz Wilkes was, without a doubt, the sexiest woman
he'd ever met. She was undoubtedly beautiful, with her
jet-black hair, her violet-blue eyes and her porcelain perfect skin. The body beneath her coveralls was distracting
enough on a daily basis. Now, dressed in a formfitting,
green bridesmaid gown that hugged every curve and ac-
centuated the full breasts and generous hips, she looked
luscious and feminine and downright sinful.

But it was more than her looks that appealed to Blake.
Jazz had more attitude than anyone he'd ever known, man
or woman. It was as if by choosing a male-dominated
profession, she'd decided to take on the sexual swagger
of a man. She was thoroughly in-your-face about her
sexuality, completely unrepentant about liking sex. A
lot. And having sex. A lot.

Part of him found that an incredible turn-on. He'd
thought about having sex with her in any number of
ways, in all kinds of places. From the floor of the han-

gar to the top of his desk to the biggest, softest bed he could find.

Another part, though—the part that wanted to punch the face of any man who was rumored to actually have had her—thoroughly disliked that side of her. He hated thinking of her with any other man, found the thought of some other guy's hand on her naked body infuriating.

He had no business feeling that way. No reason to be possessive, no excuse for jealousy. They'd never had anything other than a strict working relationship, except for the one night when he'd brought her news of her brother's disappearance.

Blake couldn't help it. He wanted her with a hunger that verged on sheer desperation. He wanted to touch her and taste her, to pound into her until the thought of every other man was driven out of her memory. Wanted to slowly make love to her until his touch was imprinted on her skin and she understood that nobody else could ever make her feel so good.

All of which was utterly impossible. Because no matter how sweet and smooth and potent it was going down, he'd still end up with one hell of a hangover once they both woke up.

Maybe when she realizes she's worth so much more....

Yeah. Maybe then. When she began to understand that she treated sex like it meant nothing because she had never cared about someone enough for it to mean anything, perhaps he could take a chance on loving her. But until then? No way in hell was he getting involved with Jazz Wilkes.

He kept that in mind as he followed her across the ballroom, trying to keep his eyes on the back of her head and not on the sway of her perfect ass beneath that formfitting satin dress.

"Jack and Coke," Jazz said as they reached the bar. Turning to him, she asked, "What's your poison?"

Blake glanced at the bartender. "The same."

"Oh, good! You didn't puss out and order white wine or something."

Damn, she was snarky. Utterly determined to unman him whenever possible. He only wondered if she had any idea why.

He knew, of course. Blake presented a challenge to her. The one man who actually wasn't interested. Or, at least, appeared not to be.

He had to keep her thinking that way. It was his only defense.

After they had their drinks, Jazz pointed to a quiet corner. He couldn't figure out what she was up to, but he knew it was something. No way had she just randomly decided to make nice with him for no reason.

Determined to keep his guard up, he followed her, until the two of them stood by a front window overlooking the veranda and front lawn. Not much of a view with the rain—although one couple had apparently decided to brave the elements. He saw a flash of emerald-green and realized one of the other bridesmaids was out there with some guy in a dark suit.

"Top shelf," Jazz said after she sipped her drink. "None of that cheap stuff. Pretty nice for an open bar."

He sipped his as well, wishing the icy-cold liquid would sluice into his veins and keep him chilled out. It was hard to stay that way when Jazz looked up at him, all moist-lipped and wide-eyed.

"So, Blake, you are staying for the costume party tonight, aren't you?"

"Yes, I plan to." He couldn't wait to see what kind of costume Jazz came up with. Knowing her, it would probably be thoroughly outrageous, driving him crazy with lust and frustration.

Hell. He should just say forget it and head back to Chicago now while he still had a brain cell left.

"You didn't get shoved over to the other hotel, did you? I mean, it would be a shame if you did—but maybe you could find somebody here with a double room you could share?"

Having heard about the mix-up with the rooms, he knew what she meant, though that twinkle in her violet eyes when she suggested *sharing* did give him pause. *What are you up to?*

"No, I actually have a room here, thanks," he said, eyeing her closely.

"Oh. Where is it?"

"Second floor."

She nodded. "I have a cottage. I guess Amanda didn't trust me in the main house. Maybe she thought I'd have wild sex and outscream her on her wedding night or something."

He sighed. "Must you?"

"Must I what, scream? Sorry, I'm a screamer. Can't help it."

"I meant, must you talk that way?"

"You criticizing my mouth?" she asked, looking both naughty and hurt all at the same time.

His mind went exactly where she wanted it to. Not that he was about to let her know that. "I'm saying you don't always have to go out of your way to be shocking.

You are capable of having just a normal conversation once in a while, aren't you?"

Jazz sucked in a quick breath, obviously surprised he'd yanked the rug out from under her. "I can when I want to," she said. Her chin went up. "I just don't happen to want to right now."

"Lucky me," he muttered.

"It could be lucky you." She licked her lips. "Like I said, I'm looking for somebody to spend the night with."

Jesus. It had finally happened. She'd stopped beating around the bush and just come out with it. He'd known she would, sooner or later. Jazz might think the way she constantly taunted and baited him was because of the way he seemed to disapprove of her. In reality, he knew it was because she felt the same sparks he did. She just didn't want to admit it—or couldn't see he returned the feeling. Heaven help him if she ever did.

"I'm not," he told her. That was true. He wasn't looking for a quick lay, as she'd put it. If and when the time came for him and Jazz, it would be about a lot more than that. Otherwise, it wasn't worth doing at all.

"Come on," she said with a small grin, "I know you're single. And so am I."

She moved a little closer, lifting a hand—so small and delicate for someone who did what she did. She brushed her fingertips across his throat, and he had to clench his teeth to avoid showing her how that slight touch affected him.

He felt it down to the soles of his feet.

"Jocelyn…"

"Look, Blake. I know we're opposites, but opposites attract, don't they? Haven't you fantasized about me, even a little?"

Get 2 Books FREE!

Harlequin® Books,
publisher of women's fiction,
presents

GET 2 BOOKS

We'd like to send you two *Harlequin® Blaze™* novels absolutely free. Accepting them puts you under no obligation to purchase any more books.

HOW TO GET YOUR
2 FREE BOOKS AND 2 FREE GIFTS

1. Return the reply card today, and we'll send you two *Harlequin Blaze* novels, absolutely free! We'll even pay the postage!

2. Accepting free books places you under no obligation to buy anything, ever. Whatever you decide, the free books and gifts are yours to keep, free!

3. We hope that after receiving your free books you'll want to remain a subscriber, but the choice is yours—to continue or cancel, any time at all!

EXTRA BONUS

You'll also get two free mystery gifts! (worth about $10)

FREE!

If offer card is missing, write to The Reader Service, P.O. Box 1867, Buffalo, NY 14240-1867 or visit www.ReaderService.com

BUSINESS REPLY MAIL

FIRST-CLASS MAIL   PERMIT NO. 717   BUFFALO, NY

POSTAGE WILL BE PAID BY ADDRESSEE

THE READER SERVICE
PO BOX 1867
BUFFALO NY 14240-9952

NO POSTAGE
NECESSARY
IF MAILED
IN THE
UNITED STATES

He was definitively pleading the fifth on that one.

"Because I've fantasized about you."

Swallowing hard, he closed his eyes briefly, then mumbled, "Knock it off, Jazz."

"Oooh, I am getting to you," she said with a grin. "You forgot to call me *Jocelyn* in that harsh, disapproving tone."

"I'm not harsh, and I don't disapprove of you," he snapped.

"Like hell."

How to explain? He couldn't. Not without telling her just how much more he wanted from her. And Jazz simply wasn't ready to hear that yet.

"I should go," he said. "The reception's breaking up."

"So how about coming back to my cottage with me for a little afternoon delight before the costume party?"

Shaking his head, he tsked. "You just don't quit."

"Not when I want something."

"Since when have you wanted me?"

She hesitated, her long, sooty lashes half lowering over her beautiful, amazing eyes. When she replied, her voice wasn't much more than a whisper. "Probably longer than I'd be willing to admit…even to myself."

She sounded serious, almost vulnerable, even. Blake's pulse pounded a little faster, his breathing hard. Because, for just a moment, he thought he was actually getting close to the real Jazz again. The woman who let her guard down once in a while, who didn't have to flaunt her sexuality because she knew she had a lot more to offer. The vulnerable girl who'd cried in his arms.

Then, just as quickly, that Jazz disappeared. Between one heartbeat and the next, that old, jaded half smile appeared on her sexy mouth and her shoulders stiffened in resolve. The moment of weakness evaporated, and it was the much more familiar Jazz who answered. "Come on, neither one of us has anything better to do. Admit it, Marshall, you know you're dying to bang me."

He let out a slow, even breath, unable to prevent a wave of disappointment from flooding over him. Jazz had disappeared behind that wall of oversexed bravado. She'd done what she always did—set out to shock and awe, never letting anybody actually get close enough to see the real woman underneath the sex-starved shell.

"Actually, Jazz, you're wrong."

She smirked. "Sure I am."

"I mean it," he said with a shrug. "Do I want to bang you? No. I don't. I really *don't*."

She stared at him, unblinking, not used to being turned down. He should have left it at that and walked away. But something—her closeness, the luminous eyes, the sweet scent rising off her skin, the warmth of her breath—made him step closer, instead. He slid one foot between hers, until their legs brushed. He could feel her thigh against his, even through her heavy dress and his pants. His arm scraped against her bare one, their chests so close he could almost feel the beating of her strong, vibrant heart.

Their mouths were just a few inches apart as he whispered, "Do I want to have sex with you? Yes."

He leaned closer, brushed his lips across her temple, rubbing his cheek in her soft hair. She said nothing, just stood there, frozen in shock.

"Do I want to make love to you? Absolutely."

This time, he heard a tiny whimper in her throat, felt her whole body sway toward him, as if the strength was running out of her legs.

"But *bang* you? Not a chance."

Blake took a step back. He immediately missed that warmth, that scent, that cocoon of wanting that had surrounded them, making him feel they were nearly invisible to the room full of people behind them.

"Come talk to me when you've grown up enough to understand the difference."

2

JAZZ WASN'T USED TO BEING turned down. Despite her reputation, she really didn't sleep around as much as some people might think, and she made a point to never approach someone she didn't already know would say yes. Having decided at a young age that love was not for her—considering most men found her a little too brash, too strong—she'd strictly set her sights on men who wanted her sexually but didn't expect anything the next morning.

At least, until today. She'd asked, and he had *not* said yes. She'd been firmly rejected.

Blake Marshall had not only said no, he'd done it in an incredibly cruel—if sensual—way. He'd given her a taste, just the tiniest glimmer of a hint of what she was missing, then insulted her by calling her immature, and walked away.

She wasn't sure which was worse. That he'd said no? Or that he'd aroused her so much first, just by moving close enough for her to get blasted by an incredible wave of testosterone.

Those lips on her forehead, the faint brush of his body—well, she had no doubt who she'd be dreaming about again tonight. Unless she had somebody else in her bed. And even then…

"Damn you," she muttered as she stared at her reflection in the mirror that evening.

Honestly, she wasn't quite sure who she was saying that to. Him, for humiliating her, and saying no? Herself, for asking in the first place?

Or Amanda—for picking out this stupid, ridiculous costume.

"A fairy-tale princess I am not," she mumbled. Stepping away from the mirror, she shook the dress, wishing she had a pair of scissors handy. She could cut off everything below the crotch and go as a pixie or something instead.

But no such luck. Not only did she have nothing with which to make any alterations, she also suspected Manda would kick her ass if she damaged this "masterpiece."

She could be on a float in the Disney Electric Light Parade. She'd pass as the offspring of lesbian lovers Snow White and Cinderella. All pale and black-haired, but wearing the most ridiculous, poofy, girly dress ever made.

It was a ball gown, pale blue, impossibly tight in the bodice, but with huge, hoop skirts at the bottom. The fabric was layered—blue satin and white lace. And the hoops were so big she would have to smooth them in every time she tried to walk through a doorway. Her four brothers—the ones who'd made her so tough and ballsy since childhood because it was the only way a tiny girl could hold her own against them—would howl with laughter if they could see her. Fortunately for her, none of them had been able to make it this weekend.

"I'll get you for this," she muttered, definitely talking to Amanda now.

Glancing at the crown, which had come with the costume, she drew the line. No way. The shoes—clear "glass" slippers made of plastic—were bad enough. No way was she wearing a freaking crown.

Actually, if she had her druthers, she would blow off this whole bash altogether. The wedding was over, as was the reception. She'd done her maid of honor bit to the best of her ability. What more could Amanda ask?

Except for her best friend to be there tonight, at what everyone knew was the *real* reception of Amanda and Reese's heart. This afternoon had been about ceremony and tradition. It had been about mollifying Amanda's uptight parents and playing the expected roles.

But tonight was about the real deal—the real couple and their life together. It was the meaningful part to anyone who really knew and loved the newlyweds.

Hell. There was no getting out of this.

Her only hope was that Blake had decided to check out and go back to the city, rather than face her again after his final crushing remark this afternoon.

Oh, she owed that man some payback. Seriously, who did he think he was talking to? Acting like he knew her better than she knew herself. As if he was absolutely sure that while she acted like she wanted wild, booty-rocking sex from any available hot body, she really wanted a great guy to give her regular, monogamous orgasms.

Like many "ogamies", monogamy was highly over-rated. She should know; she'd been there, done that, and had been on the wrong end of the teeter-totter when the guy had decided he wanted to play in another woman's playground.

Since then, Jazz had been quite happy playing the field. She'd never met a penis that wasn't just like any other, beyond size and skin tone. The bodies they were connected to were also pretty much interchangeable. Like that old movie actress—Mae West or Carole Lombard—used to say: cock-a-doodle-doo, any cock'll do.

You are such a liar.

Jazz closed her eyes, willing that voice in her head to shut up and leave her alone.

It didn't.

You know why you don't want to think of him, or any man, as anything other than a walking sex organ.

Maybe she did know. That didn't change things, though.

Jazz was just wired to have sex with men, not to actually be involved with them. Certainly not to ever be loved by them.

She'd been in love. Not once, but twice. And look where it had gotten her: Betrayed. Abused. Heartbroken. Crushed. Alone.

Never again.

Anonymous, meaningless hookups were just fine for her. And if snotty, stuck-up Blake Marshall didn't want to have one, well there would almost certainly be someone else at this party who would.

There was, of course, one problem.

Blake Marshall was the only man she wanted.

She didn't know why, didn't know how, but he had snuck up on her, worked his way in until he was all she could think about. Reflecting on it, she knew it had happened long before today. Finding him beside her this afternoon had been no accident, she'd subconsciously sought out the man. Just as she so often made excuses to go up to the front office at the airport, to happen to walk by his table when he was eating in the employees-only cafeteria. Something deep inside her had some masochistic need to get in his face. It was probably the same wicked streak that always made her try to shock him with a caustic comment or sexual jab.

Lucy to Charlie Brown. Blake, however, was not gullible enough to ever consider letting her hold the football.

God, did she hope he wasn't at the party. All this self-realization just wasn't good for her right now. And deep down, as much as she'd hated him at the time, part of her just couldn't help melting a little at the words he'd said to her this afternoon.

He wanted to have sex with her. He wanted to make love to her. He wanted more than a quick lay and a quicker goodbye.

"He does want me," she whispered, the truth of that finally hitting her, hours later.

She lowered herself to the bed, sitting quietly for a long moment, just letting herself absorb that fact.

He wanted her. Desired her. Was just as interested as she was.

But he wanted a lot more than she was ready to give right now.

Making love? She wasn't sure she even remembered how. Love hadn't been a part of her vocabulary for a good five years, and she hadn't missed it. Good riddance, in fact.

Jazz slowly shook her head, wondering when she was going to stop telling herself these wicked lies. Suddenly feeling more sad than anything else, she glanced at the clock and realized the party was already well underway. There was no more putting it off. Time to go and smile and be sassy and flirtatious and fun and never let anybody see what she was really thinking, feeling. Time to hide what she really wanted…but didn't actually hope to ever get.

Because as lovely as his words had been, at the end of the day, Blake Marshall was a man, just like every other man. Just like every other lying, betraying, heartbreaking man.

So it was better to forget he wanted her, forget she wanted him, and try to move on. Starting with the party.

Hopefully she could go in, be seen, spend an hour, then slip back out. She no longer wanted to find some anonymous guy to bring back with her, realizing that nobody she picked up would fill the empty part that had been gouged into her by Blake's impassioned words.

"Please don't be there," she whispered.

God, she hoped he wasn't. Because stiffening her resolve and reminding herself of all the reasons he was totally wrong for her would be a lot harder if she had to look into those green eyes and see the great guy she suspected was lurking inside the incredibly handsome package.

BLAKE SPOTTED JAZZ the minute she entered the room. In fact, she was impossible to miss. Studying her, he had to suck in a breath and put a steadying hand on the back of the closest chair.

Jazz was beautiful on any day of the week.

Tonight, though, she was heartbreakingly lovely.

There was a difference—subtle, maybe, but it was true. A thing could be beautiful, an object could exhibit beauty. But right now, Jazz almost glowed from within, taking his breath from his lungs and making him forget to replace it.

"Wow," said Amanda, who had been standing nearby, as happy and cheerful as only a blissful new bride could be.

"She actually wore it," said her husband, whistling a little.

Blake couldn't help asking, "Your doing?"

Amanda grinned. "Hey, she didn't make time to find a costume, so I found one for her."

"I can't believe she didn't just show up in her un-derwear and say she was coming as a Victoria's Secret model," Blake said, picturing it a little too easily.

Reese chuckled. "The night is still young."

"Don't give her any ideas!" said Amanda.

For the next half hour, Blake stayed on the far corner of the huge room, watching Jazz do her part to contribute to the party. She helped entertain, talked with just about everyone, danced a few times, had a few drinks. And, other than one single moment of eye contact, completely avoided *him*.

Eventually, though, fate, and an inebriated dance part-ner who gyrated her onto the opposite side of the dance floor, brought her right to his side. He'd been dancing with a woman from work, but immediately stiffened when he realized Jazz stood only a foot or two away, her oblivious partner still writhing against her like he intended to hump her right through her clothes.

"Hi," she said, her smile so forced he was surprised her face didn't crack.

He hated that he'd put that tension between them and wished he'd never said anything earlier. If only he'd walked away after she'd propositioned him. At least then she could still act like her normal, cocky self around him, continue flirting, not behaving as though he'd really hurt her—as if he had the power to do such a thing.

Unfortunately the tense body, too-bright smile and

too-wide eyes told him maybe he did have that power. Which shocked him. Damn.

"You look beautiful," he told her, not sure what else to say. Except, maybe, *I'm sorry I told you I want to make love with you. I should have just agreed to bang you and been done with it.*

That might have made her happy, might have given them both some sexual relief, but it would have crushed him. He knew it. He liked Jazz too much, wanted her too much, cared for her too much to go down that road.

"Thanks," she said. Then she raked a slow, thorough glance over him. She tried to remain jaded and sarcastic, but he saw the color rise in her cheeks. She was aware of him now, physically, sexually aware. It helped that his costume wasn't much like the stuffy, boring suits he usually wore at work.

When she spoke, her words lacked the sharpness she'd probably intended and her eyes continued to travel over him, as closely and intimately as a touch. "You look good, too. What are you supposed to be?"

He was wearing leather riding pants, chains, a black leather vest and fake tattoos. What the hell did she think he was supposed to be?

"He's a Hells Angel!" said Wanda, the woman he'd been dancing with. She giggled, the noise suddenly grating, though he'd always considered her a nice, if vapid thirtyish woman. "Isn't that the best? Can you imagine anybody coming in a costume more opposite than they are in real life?" Then she snickered again, this time, sounding a little less amused and a tiny bit spiteful. "Except, of course, for you, Jazz. You look positively… virginal!"

Jazz didn't so much as wince at the bitchy jab. Instead she smiled sweetly at Wanda, who wore a playboy bunny outfit that would have looked better on a woman ten years younger…and a few pounds lighter.

"I dunno, if they're handing out prizes for 'Most opposite from reality' your sexy centerfold costume has a real shot!" she said, her smile so bright and broad, Wanda didn't immediately realize she'd just been insulted.

It didn't take too long, though. A shaky smile appeared on the other woman's mouth, then it quickly faded. Her eyes hardened, even as Jazz's sparkled merrily.

Jerking her head back, Wanda looked up at Blake. "I'm so thirsty. Would you please be a sweetheart and get me a drink, honey?"

He stared at her, wondering why the hell she was acting like he was her date. He barely knew the woman. In fact, he'd only agreed to dance with her because he recognized her from work. Now she was behaving as though they'd come here together.

"Oh, don't let me interfere," Jazz said, waving a hand. She glanced over her shoulder at the inebriated dancing partner who'd been dancing behind her—a little too close behind her. "You want to go get some fresh air? It's really *stuffy* in here."

Blake tensed, watching her bat her eyes at the stranger, who couldn't take his eyes off her cleavage. She might be dressed like a sweet, virginal princess, but she also oozed sexuality. Any guy on the dance floor would see that look in her eyes as an invitation to do a lot more than get some fresh air.

Damn it, Jazz.

"You bet. I could definitely use some air. This costume is way too hot," the guy said, slurring his words a little. "Bet that dress is pretty hot, too."

In other words: *Let's get out of here and get naked.*

Jazz's smile tightened; she realized the dirty dancer might have taken her innocent invitation for a nastier one. But she didn't back down, not with Blake and Wanda standing right there. "Okay, let's go. Good to see you guys!"

Helpless to do anything else, Blake kept his eyes on Jazz as she and the guy scooted through the crowd, heading for the exit. He glanced at his watch, determined to go looking for her if she wasn't back in a few minutes. She was strong and tough and could take care of herself—but that stranger sounded like he intended to get lucky. Jazz, on the other hand, hadn't looked interested in doing anything except getting away. He wasn't sure if she had only been trying to make him jealous, or to show up Wanda. But now it looked as if she might find herself having to say no to a guy determined to hear the word yes.

Wanda, apparently remembering he was not her date, accepted another guy's invitation to dance, leaving Blake free to move closer to the door. He watched the second hand on his watch, saw it go around the dial several times.

"Five minutes," he muttered. "Time's up."

About to head outside, he stopped when he saw Jazz returning to the party…alone. Her mouth was tight, her brow furrowed. And her dress, he would swear, was slightly crooked.

His hands fisted at his sides and he strode toward her. "Are you all right?"

She glanced up, surprised. "Fine."

Looking past her, out the door, he did not see her dancing partner. "Where's your friend?"

She averted her gaze. "I don't think he was finished getting air."

"Did something happen?"

"What business is it of yours?"

"Damn it, Jazz." He grabbed her arm. "Did he hurt you?"

She shook her head. "I'm fine, Blake. Let it go. The guy's a loser."

Her voice held a hint of a tremor. Something *had* happened. Furious, he snapped, "You shouldn't have gone outside with him."

"Oh, I was asking for it, right?"

Hell, she could twist the words out of a sage's mouth. Running a frustrated hand through his hair, he said, "No. I meant, you and I both know you only went outside with him because Wanda was being catty and you still haven't forgiven me for what I said to you earlier."

Looking up at him, she licked her lips—those beautiful, kissable lips. "Are you asking me to forgive you?"

He moved closer, looking around to be sure they weren't being overheard. Jazz edged back, until she stood against the barn wall, and he followed. "Was what I said so unforgivable?"

"Only if it wasn't true."

"Then no, I can't ask for forgiveness, Jazz. Because I meant it." He lifted a hand to her face, brushed his fingertips across her soft cheek, rubbing the side of his thumb over her bottom lip. He wanted to kiss her more than he wanted to take another breath in this life. "I meant it," he repeated, his words little more than a whisper.

For a second, he thought she would wrap her arms

around his neck and draw him close for that kiss. But things were never that easy. Not with Jazz.

A deliberately cool expression crossed her face. "Well, then I feel sorry for you," she said, sliding sideways along the wall to scoot away from him. "Because you totally missed your shot and you are *never* getting another one."

<u>3</u>

THOUGH ALL SHE WANTED to do was leave, Jazz forced herself to remain at the party for another hour. She engaged in small talk, she had a drink, she nibbled on some Halloween-themed food. And she pretended to have a good time. But absolutely the only enjoyable thing about it was watching the way Amanda and Reese smiled and laughed and loved every minute of their big night.

For her, though, it was pure torture.

Torture, because, for the first time in years, she was second-guessing the choices she made. Earlier today, when Blake had made those outrageous comments about wanting to make love to her, she'd been caught unprepared, hadn't had time to react.

This time, though, when he'd admitted it was true, she'd done the one thing she didn't want to do. She'd turned him down flat and walked away.

It had been a grand and glorious exit, a great line, the kind of girl-power moment other chicks might share with their best friends.

And Jazz had regretted it one second after the words had left her mouth.

Because she *did* want Blake. She wanted to have

wild, hot sex with him, and had for a very long time. But today, after he'd turned her down so bluntly, she'd been forced to admit she wanted to make love with him, too.

It had been a long time since she'd made love with a man. A very long time. For the past several years, she'd made every effort to look at sex the same way men looked at it; the way her brothers looked at it. Hey, it worked for them, didn't it? Considering it a bodily function, an itch that could be scratched by the next available body seemed to work great for most guys she knew.

Including the two guys she'd loved. Not that she'd realized that at the time.

And it had worked for her. Or so she'd thought. At least, until lately…when it had *stopped* working for her.

It hadn't just been Blake's words. To be honest, she'd been feeling strange about her lifestyle for a few months. She'd chalked it up to not having sex for a while. A dry spell. In truth, though, she now wondered if the dry spell was the effect, not the cause. She'd stopped having sex because she'd realized it had stopped having meaning, rather than the other way around.

"I'm an idiot," she mumbled, sighing heavily over just how badly this day had gone.

Especially because, over the last hour, she'd had to watch from the other side of the room as sexy Blake Marshall danced and flirted and drank with half the other women at the party. It was as if she'd thrown a gauntlet at his feet and he'd decided to pick it up and swing it around at every horny female in the building.

It's your own fault, stupid. You should have just been honest, for once.

Honest about what she was thinking, about what she felt. Honest enough to tell him he'd been on her mind a lot lately, and that her thoughts weren't always just about having sex with him. Though, there was a lot of that.

But it was too late.

"Why are you an idiot?"

Amanda. Jazz hadn't even seen her standing close enough to overhear her crazy-person mumbling. "Just talking to myself."

"Talking to yourself, but definitely looking at someone else."

Jazz cast a quick glance at her friend, seeing that all-knowing smile. Manda was never snotty about it, and never rubbed it in, but she was almost always right. It was darned annoying. And right now, she looked like she'd just won the Final Jeopardy round with the question, "Who does Jazz want?" in response to the answer, "Blake Marshall."

"You want Blake," she said, confirming it.

"The hell you say." But the words lacked heat. Jazz couldn't even convince herself, and she sure couldn't convince her starry-eyed, love-is-in-the-air best friend.

"Oh, come on, do you really think I haven't noticed the way you've been acting around him for months? And him around you?"

"You're losing it."

Amanda crossed her arms and smirked. "Jazz, remember who you're talking to here."

She remembered. Miss-Always-Right.

"Why do you think I tried so hard to make sure he didn't get kicked to the other hotel tonight—I wanted to make sure you two had your shot."

Jazz felt her jaw drop open. "Seriously?"

"Yes, seriously." Amanda placed an arm across Jazz's

shoulders. "Look, I know you are the original man-eater, but honey, anyone who knows you at all can take one look at you and see your wandering eye has finally settled on someone at last."

She glanced across the room, saw Blake laughing with Wanda and a few others from work. She scowled. "Yeah. Someone who's not interested."

"Bullshit."

"Okay, he's interested," she admitted, "but not in the real me. He wants a nicer, gentler me."

"You are nice and gentle."

It was Jazz's turn to call bullshit.

"I mean it. You swagger and you swear and you have sex and you break hearts. But those are just things you do, not who you are."

Maybe. Perhaps Amanda was right, and there was more to her than she'd given herself credit for lately. Maybe there was even enough to deserve a guy like Blake. Maybe she'd actually grown up enough to appreciate a guy like Blake. Letting down her guard and inviting him into her real life, not just inviting him between her legs, might be the start of something special.

Or it could be the beginning of the end. The first step on a short journey to heartbreak. She just couldn't be sure.

The only thing she could be sure of was that being tough had worked for her for a long time. And old habits were hard to break.

"Would you mind terribly if I cut out for the night?" She lifted a hand to her forehead. "I really am tired and a little headachy."

Amanda looked disappointed.

"Look, I'm not saying never. Just not now," she promised. "Let me sleep on it. Hell, maybe I'll ask him to sit beside me at breakfast tomorrow."

"And at lunch, and dinner…and breakfast the next morning?"

She laughed, as Amanda had intended her to. "Who knows? I guess stranger things have happened."

Kissing the bride on the cheek, Jazz headed for the exit, keeping her stupid hoops pulled in so she wouldn't trip any poor hapless witches, devils or cheerleaders. Smiling at those she recognized, she pleaded a headache to anyone who tried to talk to her, and finally made it to the door. The on-again, off-again drizzle was on-again, but since her cottage was close, she didn't sweat it. It wasn't like she ever intended to wear this costume again, so she really didn't care if the rain ruined it.

She set off through the grass, her plastic heels slipping and sliding, then actually sinking. Tired of the costume, she stopped, bent down and pulled one shoe off.

It was probably a good thing she bent. Because stopping the way she had apparently threw off the balance of the guy who'd been following her.

The one she didn't even notice until he crashed into her and knocked her to the ground.

BLAKE HAD KEPT AN EYE on Jazz throughout the evening and had noticed immediately when she left. He hadn't tried to stop her. She looked weary and unsure, and he'd already hassled her enough for one day.

Besides, she'd made it pretty clear she wasn't interested. He'd missed his shot. Considering he hadn't wanted that shot on her terms, he really shouldn't feel so bad about it. And yet he did.

He was just about to go find Amanda and say goodnight as well when he spied the drunk guy who'd been dancing with Jazz earlier. The one she'd gone outside with and who'd come in long after she'd returned, looking more than a little annoyed. He'd been watching Jazz, moving through the crowd several feet behind her, though not speaking. And he followed her right to the door, watching from inside as she disappeared.

It might have been planned…but he didn't think so. Jazz had never been the type who needed to be sneaky about her affairs. She'd openly left with the guy earlier in the evening, so why would they need to be clandestine now?

The hairs on the back of his neck stood up. His blood surged a little harder in his veins, and he leaned forward, as if his body was warning him it was time to move. To go…somewhere.

The guy looked around the room, quickly, left then right, as if to see if anybody was watching. Then he slipped out into the night.

Son of a bitch. He was following her. Perhaps to force the issue, take what she hadn't been offering earlier tonight? Or to pay her back for turning him down—or for the way she'd turned him down?

Blake didn't know, and he didn't care. He only knew his gut was telling him Jazz was in trouble. So without a word to anyone, he strode through the crowd, moving people aside with a firm hand on a shoulder or a sharply barked word.

It was rude. He didn't care. Adrenaline pushed him onward and he was almost running by the time he got outside.

He hesitated, unsure which direction she'd gone, but only for a moment. Because, clear as a bell, he heard her voice.

"Stop it, get off me, you jerk! I said no!"

Blake swung around and took off at a run, heading toward the sound of her voice.

Ahead, he spied two figures, standing a few yards away from one of the guest cottages. He recognized Jazz instantly, the huge blue dress hard to miss. She looked like she was struggling—the guy wasn't too steady on his feet, but he had a tight grip on her. "I just want to walk you to your room," the man said, a lazy slur in his voice. "Come on, you know you want me to."

Blake didn't hesitate; he kept right on running. "Get off her, you bastard!" He plowed right into the man, sending him crashing to the wet, muddy ground. Blake landed on top of him.

"Dude, what the hell?" The guy struggled, trying to break free and rise to his feet.

Blake got there first. "You need to learn the meaning of the word no," he snarled, sending his fist in the direction of the other man's jaw. It connected with a crunch that hurt like hell but was still eminently satisfying.

"Blake, it's all right," Jazz said. "I'm all right, he didn't hurt me." She grabbed his arm, tugging him away. *"He didn't hurt me."*

"Not for lack of trying."

"He's drunk and he's stupid," she said, glaring at the other man, who was covered head to toe with mud and was now bleeding from the mouth. "Get out of here or I'll let him hit you again," she said to him.

The guy held up his hands, as if he were under arrest. "Don't, man, I'm sorry, I thought she was just playing hard to get."

"Hard to get would be a 'maybe.' A firm no, plus a knee to your groin should have clued you in to the fact that I was seriously not interested," Jazz snarled. "Now go."

The man obeyed, staggering back toward the barn. They watched him go, then Jazz whispered, "It's okay, I'm fine."

"Not for lack of trying," he shot back again, still keyed up and so on edge he felt the need to lash out.

"Excuse me?"

"Damn it, Jazz, you nearly got yourself raped all because you were mad at me."

Her eyes narrowed, practically shooting sparks. She looked furious, dangerous, with rain dripping down from her long eyelashes and her thick, black hair. "In case you didn't notice, I was taking care of him myself."

"That your way of saying thank you?"

"You…"

He shook his head, holding up a hand to stop her, then turned away. Blake needed to regain control before he said something he'd regret. Heaving in deep breaths, trying to calm his raging heart, he counted backward from a hundred.

He couldn't recall ever being so angry in his life. It had been driven purely by worry, of course—worry for Jazz. But still, he had a hard time forcing his muscles to unclench and his raging heartbeat to slow.

Finally, though, when he felt more in control, he realized he'd been way out of line. "I'm sorry," he muttered, turning back to face her. "I was afraid for you."

She didn't come back with a snappy remark, didn't cop an attitude because of the way he'd spoken to her. Instead, with quiet dignity, she murmured, "Thank you. I appreciate your help."

They stared at one another as the rain came down, harder, stinging and cold. Each drop landed on his skin, jabbing as if to punctuate that every second that ticked by was one less second he had Jazz in his arms. The

night air was cold, rich with the smells of earth and autumn, but every breath he took was filled with nothing
but her. Jazz's perfume. Jazz's breath. Jazz's skin. Jazz's
womanly arousal.

He reached out a hand. She stepped toward it.

And melted right into his arms.

"I want you, Blake," she whispered before pressing
her mouth to his in a warm, tender kiss.

He kissed her back, shocked at how good her mouth
felt—better than he'd imagined, during the many times
he'd imagined it. She parted her lips for him, licking at
his tongue, not hard and desperate, not taking control as
she so often tried to do with every part of her life. No,
this was sweet, hungry, lazy desire, not wanton lust.

Oh, lust was there, too, sluicing through him, dripping
down his body as steadily and surely as every drop of
rain. But it was all wrapped up in desire and emotion
and sensual awareness.

They kissed for a long time, rocking together, growing drenched and cold but not giving a damn.

Finally, though, she drew her mouth away from his,
kissing his cheek, then his jaw. Blake kept his arms
around her, holding her hips, filling his hands with
her.

"I want you to make love to me," she admitted,
her voice soft, small. "It's been a long time since I've
wanted that with anyone. But it's true, I want it with you,
Blake."

That was what he'd been waiting for, for so very long.
And it was all he needed to hear.

4

JAZZ WASN'T THINKING, wasn't planning, couldn't make any other decision right now if her life depended on it. But she knew she wanted Blake with every fiber of her being.

Every other night, every other lover, every other man ceased to exist. There was only him, looking at her with desire in those green eyes, as if she were the most perfect woman he had ever seen.

She wasn't going to think about tomorrow or next week or being back at work or anything else. All she wanted, for this one night, was to feel wanted and adored. To be made love to, not to be banged. To exchange long, slow kisses and caresses, to savor every inch of physical connection she could get.

"I'm sorry I was so awful to you today," she whispered. "Well, every day."

"You weren't," he told her. "You've never been awful. You've always just been sexy, sassy you."

"I think the word you're looking for is snarky."

He shook his head. "No. Never. As for today, you made me open up and be honest with you for the first time."

"Really?"

He nodded. "I've wanted you for a very long time, Jazz. I just knew I had to wait until you were ready to handle that."

"Handle…"

"Being wanted by a real man. A man who could never be satisfied with a quick lay and an easy goodbye."

Covering her lips with his, he kissed her again, deeply, exploring all the recesses of her mouth. She tilted her head, pressing hard against him, but still needed more. Feeling the hot ridge of heat pressing against her thighs, she groaned, dying to see him—all of him.

Blake lifted her by the hips and held her as she wrapped her legs around him. She ground her sex into him, quivering and almost crying with utter need.

"That's my cabin right behind us," she said, before moving her mouth to his for another deep, lazy kiss. She tangled her tongue with his, loving the way he began to slowly move it in and out of her mouth, mimicking the way he would soon move his cock in and out of her body.

Blake carried her like that—her thighs open and welcoming, her sex warm against the seam of his pants— right to her door. He only let her down so she could get the key, then followed her inside.

She reached for a light switch, flicking it on. "I want to see you," she explained.

"Likewise."

Blake remained by the door, watching as she moved toward the bed. She turned toward him, smiling and feeling wanted, desired, even though she knew she must look like a drowned rat. Thick rivulets of water ran from her drenched hair down her face. But she didn't care. She felt beautiful and wet and radiant and happy.

Reaching behind her back, she unfastened her dress and shimmied out of it, letting it fall in a big blue heap to the floor. She carelessly kicked it away, seeing the way his eyes darkened with pure appreciation as he stared at her. She'd been looked at with lust before…but oh, this was something else entirely. This was a whole new level of sexual desire, something she'd never experienced— never even dreamed of experiencing.

"My God," he whispered.

Wearing just a black bra and matching panties, she felt like woman personified. And the desire in his face only reinforced that feeling.

She walked toward him, boldly, reaching up to cup his cheek. "Touch me, please."

He did, extending a hand and cupping her waist. His strong hands teased the top curves of her buttocks as he tugged her close. They kissed again, but this time, she reached between them to unsnap the silly leather vest he was wearing. Which, to be honest, didn't look so silly when wrapped around that incredibly broad chest. The man was so much stronger than she'd ever have imagined beneath his regular clothes. His arms were thick, flexing with rippling muscle.

His chest was the same way. As she pushed the vest off, she stepped back to look at him, fascinated by the swirl of dark hair surrounding his flat nipples. It thickened a little, then trailed down in a thin line over his flat belly, disappearing into his pants.

When she reached for those pants, he put his hand on hers. "Huh-uh."

She pouted.

"Slow and delicious," he told her, leaning down to kiss her again.

Yeah. Slow and delicious could work.

Blake unfastened his pants, letting them hang open, and she pressed hard against him. The man was huge and rock-hard. She didn't look down, wanting to keep her eyes closed like a kid on Christmas morning, knowing the surprise was going to be so much better than anything she could possibly imagine.

"Please," she whispered, rubbing her breasts against his chest, "I need…"

He understood. Blake reached around and unhooked her bra with a flick of his fingers, then stepped back enough for her to let it fall away from her breasts. He let out a low groan at the sight of her, then pushed her back until her legs hit the bed.

Spinning around, so he was the one sitting on it, he drew her close, then kissed the bottom curve of one breast. She shivered, arching toward his mouth, but he teased her, kissing everywhere but on the sensitive tip. Finally he took mercy and lifted his hand to her other breast, tracing the tips of his fingers over her nipple.

She gasped at the pleasure of it. But it still wasn't enough. Twining her hands in his hair, she silently begged him to taste her. To make her *feel*.

He seemed to sense her desperation and moved his mouth to her nipple, kissing her, licking, nibbling. Then finally, at last, sucking deeply.

Her legs gave way. She collapsed onto his lap, parting her legs to straddle him. He still wore his pants and boxer briefs, and she had her panties on, but that enormous cock fit delightfully against her sex. She stroked it, up and down, riding him through their clothes as he pleasured her breasts until she was sobbing.

"Please, Blake," she said, "let me touch you."

He didn't resist as she pulled away, standing up again and drawing him up before her. Biting her bottom lip, she reached for his pants, pushing them down over his lean hips. The boxer briefs strained to contain his cock, and she held her breath, reaching out to brush her fingers against a spot of moisture on the cotton fabric.

When she brought her finger to her mouth and tasted his essence, he sucked in a sharp breath. "Wicked."

"You have no idea how wicked I can be."

"You're wrong about that."

"Okay, I guess you have some idea."

But she intended to thoroughly prove it to him, to leave him with absolutely no doubt.

Jazz tugged the briefs out of the way, gasping as she saw that big, thick erection. All her feminine parts went even more soft and slick at the thought that she'd soon have all of that inside her.

He didn't let her push his clothes all the way off, as if not trusting himself to let her put her hands on him.

Hmm. She wondered how he'd feel about her mouth.

Deciding to find out, she pushed him back onto the bed as soon as his clothes hit the floor. "Lie down," she ordered.

He gave her a warning look, but she ignored it. Bending toward him, she kissed his flat abs, tasting the ridges of muscle, dipping her tongue into his belly button, then moving lower.

"Jazz," he groaned.

"Let me," she begged.

He didn't refuse her. Which she took as a yes.

Jazz had always liked oral sex. She liked getting it, and she liked the utter helplessness a man seemed to experience when he was getting it. But this was different. She wanted him in her mouth because she wanted to please him. His pleasure was foremost on her mind.

There was no calculation, no gamesmanship, no who's-on-top control issues.

She flicked her tongue out, licking at the thick head, tasting more of that moisture. He jerked when she blew on his skin, and cried out when she covered the tip of his cock with her lips.

Kissing, sucking lightly, she opened her mouth wider, taking a little more. Then a little more. He filled her, and she absolutely adored the fullness. Almost as much as she adored the taste—and the sound of his helpless pleasure.

"Jazz," he groaned, twining his hands in her hair.

She couldn't answer verbally, so she took more, swallowing as much of his cock as she could take. Then she pulled away, making slow, careful love to him with her mouth. He caught her rhythm and though he tried desperately to remain still, she knew by the instinctive thrusts of his hips that he was holding on by a thread.

"Enough!" he finally said, grabbing her shoulder and physically pulling her off.

She pouted. "I liked it."

"I liked it, too. But you know what I like better?"

She was almost afraid to ask—afraid it wouldn't be what she hoped it was.

"I like this," he snapped, flipping her onto her back. He reached for her panties, yanked them down, kissed his way up her thigh toward her aching core.

Oh, yes, it was what she'd hoped it was.

"Oh, please!" she cried when he moved close to the lips of her sex.

"Not yet," he told her, "I want to look at you first."

He sounded as if he'd never seen anything so pretty as her freshly waxed sex, bare but for the tiny tuft of curls at the very top. A painful process, but so worth it if only for the look on this man's face at this very minute.

"I somehow knew you'd look like this."

She writhed on the bed, arching toward his mouth. "Oh?"

"Uh-huh. Knew you'd be nice and smooth, just perfect against my lips and tongue."

"Prove it," she ordered, frustration welling up inside her.

He laughed softly, then kept kissing her thigh, letting his slightly roughened cheek brush against her, occasionally blowing out a low breath that made her shake.

Only when she was a writhing, begging mess did he give in and dip his mouth to her clit. When he sucked it between his lips, she bucked on the bed. "Yes!"

He ignored her, holding her hips with his big, strong hands as he licked her into insanity. He sucked and kissed her to the edge of orgasm, then moved down, slipping his tongue between the lips of her sex and licking all the way into her opening.

She couldn't help it. A low, quivery cry escaped her mouth and she began to shake. He moved again, going back to that throbbing nub, and this time, he didn't let up until she'd screamed out as a rollicking orgasm gripped her and thrashed her around on the bed.

She had barely stopped screaming when he moved up her body, kissing her tummy, her midriff, her breasts, the hollow of her throat and her neck. Finally he reached her face and pressed his mouth to hers. She wrapped her arms around his neck, holding him close, kissing him deeper.

Parting her thighs for him, she whispered, "I'm on birth control. And, uh, despite my reputation, I promise you have nothing else to worry about." Frankly

her reputation wasn't nearly as bad as some people—
Wanda—might think.

"Same here," he told her.

Then there was no more talking. He slid the tip of his
cock into her, easing in, making sure she was comfort-
ably taking every inch before he gave her another.

There were a lot of inches. So many she was gasping
by the time he buried himself to the hilt inside her.

"Okay?"

She nodded, unable to speak.

"You sure?"

"Hell, yes, I'm sure," she promised. Then she lifted
her legs higher, feeling him shift so deep he touched her
womb.

She cried out again in utter bliss.

Seeming to realize she was loving this, and in no way
in pain, Blake appeared to throw off his last restraints.
Grabbing one of her legs, he looped it over his shoulder
so he could drive even deeper. Jazz writhed, taking and
taking, then giving back, meeting thrust after thrust.

At some point, they rolled over and she was on top,
riding him hard and fast, loving the way he looked up
at her. He smiled broadly, playing with the wet hair that
stuck to her sweaty face. He appeared fascinated by
the way her breasts bounced with her every move. He
cupped them, tweaking, stroking, pinching a little, and
she was hit with another orgasm.

She straightened, cried out, feeling all her muscles
clench. Then, as soon as it released her, focused on
him—getting him there, too.

Seeing her like that seemed to have done the trick.
Blake's eyes were closed, he was panting and thrusting
wildly. But before he came, he turned her over again,

wrapping his arms tightly around her, burying his face in her hair.

"You're beautiful, Jazz," he told her. "So damned beautiful. And I've wanted you forever."

Then, with a final cry of pleasure, he came inside her, taking her over the top with him for a third and final time.

JAZZ HADN'T SPENT an entire night in bed with a man for a long time. In recent years, her bed-partners had not been the stay-the-night type, nor had she wanted them to be.

Last night, however, she hadn't minded. In fact, she'd loved it. If Blake had gotten up and started pulling on his clothes after making such amazing love to her—twice—she probably would have cried.

But he hadn't. He'd stayed curled up with her in the bed, throughout the long rainy, lovely night, whispering to her, touching her, making love to her, giving her more pleasure than she thought any person was capable of receiving.

Now, though, it was morning. Dawn's watery light was streaking through the window blinds. And with the dawn came day. With day, reality.

What that meant for them, she didn't know.

She'd done what he'd wanted. She'd let him make love to her. Now she wondered if she would live to regret it, as she had the only other times she'd truly let down her guard and opened her heart.

Oh, God, your heart? Are you kidding?

No, actually, she didn't think she was. She truly feared her heart had opened to Blake that night her brother had gone missing, when he'd been so strong and tender. And he'd sailed right into it sometime during yesterday and last night, when he'd made it so clear he thought she was worth a lot more than a quick lay and a quicker goodbye.

"What's wrong?" he asked, as if sensing she'd grown distracted.

She hesitated.

"Jazz?"

Not used to sharing her feelings or any of that gushy stuff, she considered making a flip remark, then seducing him again. That might get by the heavy moment, then they could go to breakfast, head back to the city, hopefully get together again soon and…what?

They'd burn out. He'd pull away. If she didn't let him all the way in, she knew that's what would happen.

She had to take a chance.

"You know what I said last night, about not being quite as experienced as some might think?"

He nodded.

"It's true," she said. "Not that I'm some wilting flower, believe me. But I don't sleep around quite as much as you might think."

"I don't think anything, Jazz. I don't really want to think anything about the past, who you've been with, who I've been with. I just want to move forward. With you."

She liked the sound of that. Moving forward together.

"I'd like that, too," she admitted. "But I don't know that it will happen unless I explain some things to you."

He curled his head under the pillow, so lazy-man-in-the-morning sexy, watching her with sleepy green eyes. "Like what?"

She licked her lips, twirling the bedsheet in her hands.

"It's okay," he told her, grabbing one hand. "You can say anything to me. It's not going to change how I feel about you."

How he felt about her? That was part of the problem—she didn't know how he felt about her. She knew he wanted her, knew he desired her, knew he intended for this to continue after they left this room. Emotionally, though, she just wasn't sure where he stood.

"I was a sweet, innocent little virgin once, you know." Seeing his brow shoot up, she added, "And I don't mean when I was fourteen."

"I didn't say a word."

She continued. "I have four older brothers and over-protective parents. Believe me, I was the textbook straight-and-narrow good girl until I went away to college."

"And then?"

"And then I fell in love," she admitted. "Madly in love with a guy named Chuck."

He rolled his eyes.

"Yeah, I know. Chuck. Yuck. The point is, I loved him with all of my nineteen-year-old heart."

"And he broke it."

"Oh, big-time."

He reached over and brushed a strand of hair off her face. "I'm sorry."

He was, she could see that. But every nineteen-year-old girl got her heart broken, she knew that. She hadn't quite made her point.

"After Chuck, I stayed single for a long time, then when I was twenty-two, I fell in love again. This time, I was sure it was the real deal. He proposed, I was wearing his ring, we moved in together, I was picturing the three-bedroom split level and babies. He was picturing…"

"Something else?"

"Every other woman he could get his hands on," she admitted, surprised that the admission still had the power to hurt her so many years later. Not that she pined for her ex-fiancé. Last time she'd heard a word about him, it had been that he was a used car salesman on his second marriage, paying child support to two different women. Loser with a capital L.

But thinking about the betrayal still stung. Thinking about walking into the apartment they'd shared and finding him in bed with another woman still ripped at her guts.

She didn't like talking about it, but finally, with Blake, she felt she could.

So she did. She told him the whole story. Told him how she'd felt at that moment, and how she'd reacted. Told him why she'd taken solace in the arms of a bunch of different men, until she'd begun to think every single one was just the same. This time, she was the one who loved 'em and left 'em, the one who really didn't care if the guy she was hooking up with was single or not. She'd been hurt and broken, now she did the hurting and the breaking.

Throughout her entire recitation, Blake watched her, quietly, only occasionally nodding or reaching out to touch her hand or her cheek.

Finally she was finished. She'd said all she had to say, revealed her deepest secrets, her darkest moments, her self-doubts. The only other person she'd ever told these things to was Amanda, and she'd had romantic problems of her own.

Once done, she felt drained, wrung-out, but glad to have laid things out on the table. Because if there really was something more here than desire, more than lust, more than a lay and a quick goodbye for them, now was the time to find out. And telling him the truth was the surefire way to see where she stood.

He didn't say anything for a while. He merely looked at her, touched her. Then, finally, he offered her a half smile and drew her closer, wrapping her in his arms.

"Jazz? Do you think you're finished with all that now?"

It wasn't what she had expected. She'd been prepared for questions, maybe even a judgmental glance. Not this casual acceptance. Not this…kindness.

"Yes," she told him, speaking truthfully, "I think I could be finished with it. It's not easy for me to trust, to let down my guard. But I think it's possible."

"You can trust me," he whispered. "I promise you, I will never do anything to hurt you, if it's within my power to avoid it."

That was about as much as any person could ever promise, wasn't it?

"I believe you."

He nodded once. "Okay then. It's done."

"Just like that?"

"Just like that."

Their stares met, locked, and she wondered if it could really be that easy. Could a bad reputation and a jaded attitude really be swept away by one passionate, loving night and the kindness of one single, amazing man?

He pulled her toward him and kissed her mouth, sweetly, tenderly.

And she began to suspect that yes, it could indeed.

LATER THAT MORNING, when they set out to walk to the inn for the wedding breakfast, Blake found himself marveling over how his life had changed in just eighteen hours. He'd driven out here from Chicago yesterday carrying a big torch for a woman who he'd hoped would one day get around to calming down and really seeing him as a man, rather than a conquest.

Now that woman was walking beside him, her hand clenched in his, wearing a smile so bright it rivaled the sun that had finally begun to peek out through the clouds.

He didn't fool himself that things would be easy, or perfect. But he already knew one thing: he was in love with Jocelyn Wilkes. Crazy in love. He had been for a long time; she'd just been too prickly to let him show it.

Now, honestly, he simply couldn't help himself.

He lifted her hand to his mouth and kissed it. "Do you have a ride back to Chicago?"

She nodded. "A limo is supposed to take everyone back."

"How about riding with me on my bike?"

She lifted a brow, looking up at him in surprise.

"You don't think I'd dress up as a biker if I didn't really have a bike, did you?"

"You? Seriously?"

"Come on, after last night, are you saying you still haven't shaken this picture you have of me as some boring P.R. guy?"

She smiled like a cat holding a canary. "Mmm. Nope, not boring. Not straitlaced. You have a very naughty side, Mr. Marshall."

"Well, that's only fair, considering you have a very *nice* one, Miss Wilkes."

Casting him a mock glare, she shook a finger at him. "Don't you dare tell anyone. That's one reputation I'll never live down."

"It'll be our secret, my love."

She stopped suddenly, freezing midstep on the lawn. Turning to face him, the laughter faded from her face and those violet eyes were searching, questioning. "What did you call me?"

He shouldn't say it. He knew it was too soon, that she wasn't ready, that he'd come across as crazy for being this sure, this soon.

But he couldn't lie to her. Couldn't look into that beautiful face without telling her how he really felt.

"I called you my love," he admitted.

She bit her lip.

Blake slid his arms around her waist and pulled her to him. "Don't chicken out on me now, Jazz."

"I'm not chickening out."

"Good. Because I love you."

He felt her stiffen for a moment, saw her mouth tremble. She stared wildly around, as if poised to flee.

"I love you. And you're okay with that," he insisted.

"I am?"

"Yeah. You are."

She hesitated for one more moment. Then, at last, nodded. A smile appeared, tiny, tentative, and she whispered, "I am."

Rising on tiptoe, she brushed her mouth against his. She didn't say the words back to him. He knew they wouldn't come easy to her lips. But as she looked into his face, her expression said it anyway.

She loved him. Someday, she'd say it.

And he was a patient enough guy to wait for her.

* * * * *

Last Call

_1_

PLEASE NOT ME, *please not me, please not me.*

The mantra repeated in Abby Bauer's head, but it didn't help. Because, like an arrow shot from an expert marksman's bow, the bridal bouquet was headed straight for her. In fact, if Abby wasn't sure her sister didn't like Keith—Abby's fiancé—she'd suspect Amanda's over-the-shoulder aim had been intentional.

A bunch of other single women surrounded her at the base of the sweeping, curved staircase, a dozen steps below the bride. Each appeared ready to claw out someone's eyes in order to catch a stupid clump of tea roses cupped in baby's breath—like it was made out of diamonds or something. They elbowed each other, shrieking with laughter, jumping and reaching up so high a few in strapless dresses risked a wardrobe malfunction.

But no. The damn thing didn't so much as come close to another woman's updo. It was on a collision course with Abby Bauer's face.

She acted quickly, almost without thinking. Flinging up an arm, she backhanded the bouquet to the right, passing it like a volleyball player would set up a team-mate's kill-shot.

"I got it!" shrieked a young woman Abby didn't know—one of the ones in a strapless dress. She hadn't popped a boob while clawing for the bouquet, but she was on the verge of doing so now, by jumping up and down. "I'm so excited!"

Yeah, and the men would be really excited if those Ds defied gravity and separated from her dress midleap. But maybe that wouldn't be such a bad thing. Because it would certainly provide a distraction from what she had just done.

She, a supposedly happily engaged woman, had batted a good-luck, next-to-be-married bridal bouquet like it was a giant flying cockroach.

"Maybe nobody noticed," she mumbled under her breath, almost scared to look around to see.

Maybe Keith had gone outside. To, uh, smoke. Only he didn't smoke. But maybe he'd wanted some air. Some cold air. Cold, wet, stormy air. And maybe his parents—and hers—had gone with him.

Because coldness suited every last one of them so very well.

Not Keith. At least, not the Keith she'd met and fallen in love with…the one so seldom in evidence these days.

Taking a deep breath, she shifted her gaze to the right. All the men, and the non-single females—or the simply non-desperate ones—had gathered in the reception room right off the foyer, to watch the standard wedding tradition through the arched doorway.

At the left edge of that archway stood Mrs. Manning, her future mother-in-law. The woman oozed disapproval. Her face seemed like it had been slathered with one of those facial mud-masks that had completely dried and was ready to crack apart into a million pieces. Tight. Hard. Brittle.

This wasn't good.

Next to Mrs. Manning stood her husband. The naturally deep frown on his brow had delved to crater depths, his pugnacious jaw thrust out and his chest even more so.

This *so* wasn't good.

Next to him? Abby's own prim, proper mother, whose eyes were saucer-size in her pale face. Upset didn't quite describe the expression. Scandalized was about as close as she could get.

Okay, this was bad.

Standing behind his wife, a hand on her shoulder, gripping her as he acknowledged how much Abby had just embarrassed him in front of the Mannings, was her father. He wore the fiery glare he usually reserved for Amanda, the "wild child" of the family.

Extremely bad.

But she didn't realize it was an utter calamity until she looked to the other end of the wide arch. Her stare immediately locked with the dark brown eyes she most didn't want to see.

Keith. Her fiancé. Looking a little stunned. And maybe, she realized with a twist of her heart, a bit hurt.

Oh, God, what have I done?

"Okay, it's time for the garter," someone shouted.

Abby quickly looked away, trying to calm her racing heart and smooth her choppy breaths. Thankful for the interruption, she turned her attention to the bride and groom. Reese, her new brother-in-law, was already on one knee on the stairs, lifting Amanda's dress with smooth, sexy determination.

All the women swooned a bit. Including her. Because the newlyweds were so erotically charged together, they made everyone else feel inadequate somehow.

"I want one," wailed the girl who'd caught the bouquet. Whether she meant a husband, or a man who could make stroking another woman's calf look absolutely orgasmic, Abby didn't know.

Funny, Abby wanted one, too. Oh, not a husband, at least, lately she hadn't. But a man who'd get on his knees and touch her with utter sensuality in front of a huge crowd of people, because he was so wildly in love with her and desired her that much. What woman *wouldn't* want that? Especially if she'd never had it—and feared she never would.

"Come on, big guy, you can do it. Take it off," Amanda purred, sultry laughter in her voice as Reese continued tugging the lacy garter down her leg. With his teeth.

Double swoon.

Once the garter was off Amanda's thigh and looped around her husband's finger, Reese stood and waved it at the crowd. The bouquet-hungry women moved away, making room for single men who would jockey to catch the frilly clump of lace. Abby trudged with them, finally working up the nerve to look at her fiancé again.

He stood in the same position. Silent. Still. Intense.

God, the man was handsome. Probably the handsomest one here. Everywhere they went, women's eyes were drawn to his dark brown hair, his sculpted face, full mouth, strong jaw. Tall and lean, he wore his expensive tailored suit as easily as most men wore jeans. Keith could be posing on magazine covers rather than working as a corporate lawyer. Her fiancé was everything a woman would want. And she'd wanted him, too. Desperately. Raised in a cold, passionless house, she'd held this secret, fairy-tale hope of someday falling wildly in love with her own Prince Charming. Despite the odds, despite her parents inattentiveness, she'd truly believed in happily-ever-after. Heck, it was why she'd become an event planner, because she so loved weddings, loved that moment when everything was shiny and beautiful and new and absolutely every couple was sure to make it.

That half of them didn't was something she wouldn't even contemplate. On that one day, anything was possible.

Yes, Abby Bauer, the "good" sister, the quiet, proper, nice one, was just a silly little romantic at heart. And Keith, handsome corporate attorney Keith Manning, had once seemed exactly like her perfect Prince Charming.

So what happened?

Good question. Honestly, she didn't know. Sometimes, he still seemed like that perfect man. When he let his guard down and stared at her with that wistful, tender expression, or when he whispered something sweet to her, when he dropped a possessive arm across her shoulders, she still felt certain he was madly in love with her.

Other times, though, she just wasn't so sure. And it was hard to fantasize about a happily-ever-after with even the most perfect of Prince Charmings if you weren't totally sure he was wildly, deeply in love with you, too.

Keith watched as she drew closer. Even from several feet away, Abby witnessed the moment his initial look of surprise—and hurt—gave way to a much more familiar cool, detached expression. He retreated behind the formal mask he almost always wore, except when they were alone. Which seldom happened anymore.

Where are you? Where did you go? Why won't you let me see the real you anymore?

She didn't know. So, with a sigh, she kept trudging.

Her parents and the Mannings bore down on her as soon as she reached the archway. "Abigail!" her mother snapped.

"What is *wrong* with you?" asked Mrs. Manning.

But before anyone could truly begin to berate her, Keith took her by the arm, holding firmly, staring down both sets of parents. "If you'll excuse us, Abby and I want to get a look at the grounds," he said, his tone even.

Mr. Manning and her father exchanged a glance. Then both nodded in approval, as if imagining Keith would take her outside to set her straight, ensuring she never embarrassed him in public again. She didn't suspect he would do any such thing, but the older generation obviously felt she deserved it. Lord, she felt like a fifteen-year-old schoolgirl caught between her parents and the school principal.

"Shall we?" Keith asked her.

She nodded, relieved, even though she'd just been thinking about how cold and rainy it was. "Great idea."

Keith led her away from the crowd, toward the French doors at the back of the reception hall—once a ball-room in the grand old house. With every step, she felt the weight of four pairs of angry eyes boring into her back.

Unable to help it, she cast a quick look back over her shoulder. Yep. Still staring. Still disapproving. Still so damned cold.

"Don't worry about them," he ordered in a low voice. "It's nobody else's business."

She had to wonder what he meant by "it." Them? Their relationship? Their engagement? Or the way she'd just reacted to a symbol that predicted a quick marriage for her.

They didn't say another word until they were outside on the veranda, alone. On a nicer day, the event would probably have spilled out here, but the drizzle and gusty winds kept everyone else indoors. Funny how much the grayness and the chill suddenly suited her mood.

"Cold?" he asked, obviously seeing her shiver a little.

"Yes, but that's not such a bad thing. I was starting to feel suffocated in there."

In so many ways.

"Me, too," he admitted. Then he slipped out of his suit jacket and draped it over her shoulders. "But it is pretty cool."

"Thank you," she murmured as his strong fingers brushed her skin. The heat of them was so stark against the cold day, she shivered again.

His hands didn't linger, not now, not when there was a chance someone could come outside. As usual when they weren't entirely alone, he remained impersonal. Whether carefully taking her arm when they walked, or dancing a few inches away at some social event, or greeting her with a chaste kiss on the cheek when they met for dinner, Keith always maintained that impeccable protocol. Not to mention a few inches of space. Not unkind, not unfriendly, but ever-so-proper.

Sometimes she found it hard to believe the same hands could do such amazing things to her body.

Not often. Not recently.

But oh, God, had he given her pleasure beyond imagining on occasion. With his intimate touch, the man had worked utter magic on her, nearly always without taking any for himself. As if he were addicted to the feel and taste of her body, he'd worshipped her for hours, only gaining his own satisfaction when she absolutely insisted on it. Even then, he had rarely wanted intercourse, swearing he was satisfied with her hand.

Well, she wasn't. Damn it, she *wasn't*. And if he was telling the truth, and that was really all he wanted, then she feared her fiancé was every bit as passionless as his parents—and hers. Which was too depressing to contemplate.

Wrapping the coat tightly around her body, she steeled herself against a rush of instinctive pleasure as his warm, masculine scent surrounded her. She didn't want to be vulnerable right now, sensing the conversation she was about to have would be a very important one—even though she had no idea what he was thinking. The man was so inscrutable, she couldn't tell if he was offended, angry, or amused.

Well, amusement was probably a stretch.

When he did speak, he sounded merely pragmatic. "You have cold feet."

She didn't even pretend to misunderstand, or joke that her toes were numbing up as moisture soaked into her shoes from the wet wood planking. "I suppose I do."

"Perhaps you could have said something, rather than taking it out on a poor bunch of flowers?"

That could have been teasing, if there'd been the least hint of humor. But his voice remained emotionless, his expression revealing absolutely nothing.

God, that passionless stoicism drove her absolutely crazy. It might be perfect for his job as a lawyer for a major international corporation, but here, between them, it was utterly maddening. "Maybe I *have* been by not wanting to name a date, or start planning anything," she snapped. "Maybe the problem is that none of you have heard me."

Keith frowned. "*None* of *us?* I thought I was the groom."

"Right. So when's the last time you looked at an invitation sample or checked out a photographer's work or anything having to do with a wedding?"

He shifted uncomfortably. "You know I'm not good at that stuff. It's what you do for a living, you're the expert."

Maybe it was a guy thing, and maybe he had a point. Still, she had been bothered that, lately, she and Keith never talked about their wedding, or their relationship, or anything personal at all. His aloof, self-controlled wall seemed to have grown with every month that passed, until they'd gotten into a two-dinners-a-week routine that was so bloody boring and predictable, she wanted to scream about it. "Yes, I'm the expert. But I would think you'd have a little interest."

"You're right, I'm sorry. I just figured it was a woman's thing."

"Spoken just like your father would say it," she said. *Or mine.*

"I'm sorry," he said, sounding as though he meant it.

She was in no mood to make up. "Or your mother. I mean, God knows, the wedding is all I ever hear about from her, and it's only gotten worse. I get a weekly phone call from her with a lecture demanding to know why I can find time to help Manda, or my clients, with their weddings and not plan mine." Frankly she'd always considered it a little like the cobbler's children going without shoes—there just didn't seem to be enough time in the day. Lately, though, she'd begun to wonder if, deep down, there wasn't more to it.

He was silent for a moment, then he turned and glanced at the grounds, his handsome, masculine profile still making her heart skip a beat. Though wet, the gold and orange autumn leaves provided a beautiful backdrop and the lawn still held a hint of summer lushness. He stared intently at it for the longest time. Then, finally, he cleared his throat, but he didn't look her way.

"Actually that's a good question, Abby. I think I'd like to know the answer myself. Why did you have so much time to devote to your sister's wedding, and none to ours?"

This time, there was something in the tone. Something that told her he'd been more bothered by what she'd done than his first response had indicated. As if she'd finally pierced that shell and was again speaking to at least the remnants of the man she'd fallen in love with. The one hidden beneath that withdrawn exterior—who she hadn't seen in so long she hardly remembered what he was like.

The one who deserved an honest answer.

"It *is* a good question, Keith," she said, her heart breaking as she admitted the truth, to both of them, for the very first time. "I suppose the answer is because I don't really want to marry you."

HEARING HER ADMIT IT, hearing the woman he loved with every ounce of his being say she didn't want to marry him, was easily the worst moment of Keith Manning's life. Feeling as though she'd kicked his legs out from under him, he had to clutch the railing, holding so tightly, wet splinters of wood dug into his palms.

He'd lost her. He'd lost, *period*. For the first time, ever.

The enormity of that stunned him into silence.

He'd never failed to get something he truly wanted. And he'd wanted Abby from the day they'd met—when she'd come to plan a fund-raising event for the law firm where he worked. Only after he'd gotten to know her did he realize she was every bit as beautiful inside as she was outwardly.

He'd fallen so hard it had scared the hell out of him. Keith had never felt anything like it, had never been a slave to his emotions. He'd always figured he'd meet a decent woman who fit into his lifestyle and shared his goals, and they'd settle down into a convenient partnership with respect and mutual admiration. That was the way every other marriage he'd ever seen—from his parents to his colleagues—had been.

But Abby? Abby made his blood boil.

She made him wild with lust, with her almost exotic, dark eyes, her long, silky brown hair, her lithe body and her subtle laugh. She made him so crazy with wanting he had to fight a constant inner battle not to back her into the nearest corner and take her in rough, animalistic passion.

He'd never done it. Abby was gentle and quiet, not very experienced. She came from a reserved background. She had this belief in a happily-ever-after, wanted a Prince Charming who'd treat her with respect. That's exactly what he wanted to be to her. And Prince Charming, as far as he recalled, had never dragged Cinderella into the nearest broom closet and screwed the glass slippers right off her feet.

He'd always respected women, of course, but those he'd had affairs with had seemed fine with the kind of steamy sex he was into. But he'd been raised to believe a wife was different, and he damn well *knew* Abby was. So he'd restrained himself, kept his basest desires in check, because the last thing he'd ever want to do is hurt her, or repulse her. He'd been what had been drilled into his head for his entire life, and given her exactly what he'd thought she wanted at the same time: a complete gentleman.

Apparently for nothing. He'd somehow managed to scare her off, anyway. "You're serious?"

"Yes."

It was all he could do to control the roiling emotions surging through him as he heard the finality in her voice and realized it was over, that he'd never have her the way he'd always wanted to. That she wouldn't be his wife. His lover. Or the mother of his children.

He'd lost. And for the life of him, he didn't know why. How could he lose when he'd played the game by every single one of her romantic rules?

Only a lifetime's worth of training at the hands of two rigid, emotionless parents and the presence of a hundred people in the room just beyond the closed doors kept him from dropping to his knees and begging her to tell him what he'd wrong, to give him the chance to make it right. Instead he released the rail, dropped his hands to his sides and turned again to face her.

Abby's beautiful face was tear-streaked, her mouth trembling the slightest bit. Yet there was resolution there. He saw it in the squared shoulders, the uplifted jaw. She meant it.

Still, he had to ask, "You're not in love with me anymore?"

She sucked in an audible breath, and her throat

quivered as she swallowed. "I don't want to marry you, Keith."

She'd avoided the question. Not that it seemed to matter since the end result was the same: no Abby in his life. "So this is it? It's over? We're finished?"

A brief hesitation, a searching glance, then she nodded. "Yes. I think we are."

"Just like that."

"It's been building to this for a long time," she said softly, "and I think we both know it."

He managed not to laugh at himself. Because, no, he had not known it. Sure he had sensed Abby's distraction, maybe a little withdrawal. But he'd figured it was work, or stress, her obnoxious parents—or his. He'd never imagined she'd changed her mind about him... *them.*

She reached for the sparkling engagement ring he'd flown to New York to buy for her. But Keith waved a hand. "Keep it."

It had been specially made for her. No other woman could ever wear it. That would break his heart beyond all repair.

"I can't do that," she insisted. "It wouldn't be right."

"I don't want it," he said, staring at her from three feet away, feeling like it was three thousand. His openhearted Abby had suddenly become a stranger—an aloof, distant stranger.

"It's the principle..."

"Look, if you don't want to wear it, fine. But I have no use for it. Donate it to charity or something, I don't care." He glanced toward the reception hall. "Though, actually, you should keep it on for a while. I'm sure you don't want to spoil your sister's day. If everybody finds out, an argument could break out. My parents will be angry, yours will be put in the position of having to defend you."

"They wouldn't," she said quietly. "Defend me, I mean. They certainly never have before. I have no doubt they'll find this indefensible."

He stared, unable to read her, but certain of one thing: Abby had changed. She had never said anything disloyal about her family, which had always shocked him, to be honest. Because, as parents went, hers were almost as crappy as his.

"I'll break it to them after the reception and we'll go," he offered. "I'm sure you don't want us sticking around for the party, anyway."

"I somehow doubt they were looking forward to it."

Maybe not. But he had been. Very much.

Yes, she'd picked out a stupid Roman warrior type costume for him. But seeing her as a Grecian goddess would have made it worthwhile. He'd looked forward to dancing with her, holding her in his arms—even though he couldn't hold her tightly for fear he'd lose his head, do or say something to reveal his wild need, to offend or frighten her. To somehow fall off that princely pedestal and let her see that he was just a guy, just an average, normal, horny guy who was so racked with hunger for her, he had a hard time keeping a sane thought in his head.

The realization that he'd never hold her again had him ready to throw back his head and howl.

"All right. Thank you." Then she turned toward the door. "I should go. The reception will be ending soon."

He almost let her, was about to watch her walk away,

with quiet dignity, which, he knew, was what a real man *should* do.

Be strong, be stoic, never show your emotions. Words he'd learned to live by from a very young age. Words that had been reinforced throughout his law school days and his legal career.

But he just couldn't let her go without some kind of explanation. Maybe it would be hurtful, but he still had to know. So he stepped closer, lifted his hand and pressed it flat on the closed door.

Swallowing hard, knowing he was going to sound too damn needy but unable to help it, he simply asked, "Why?"

She tilted her head to look up at him, surprise widening her brown eyes a tiny bit. Then, shaking her head in visible sadness, she answered. "Because I don't want the kind of life I can see spread out before me. I want what Amanda has with Reese—freedom, excitement. Pure passion."

He sucked in a breath, so shocked, he dropped his hand.

"You're a good man, Keith," she said. "A wonderful man. But the truth is, I want someone who'd have no problem falling to his knees and tugging a garter off my leg in front of a hundred people without a second thought. One who would actually kiss me in public. One who'd fly to Vegas and play hooker-and-john with me, no matter who found out."

His head spun and he had trouble focusing. He'd heard the story about her sister Amanda's embarrassing YouTube incident, when she and her fiancé had gotten caught on camera playing a sexy game in Las Vegas. In fact, he'd heard it from Abby's shocked mother, and had naturally assumed Abby had been just as shocked.

Even though he, himself, had found it funny as hell. Not to mention exciting.

She went on. "You're gorgeous and you're charming and you're everything a woman could want. But, I'm sorry, I want a husband who doesn't consider me part of his regular, daily routine. Who isn't content to provide me with an occasional orgasm just so he can check them off his to-do list, and then go back to work."

Keith's heart raced and he actually staggered back.

"I want to marry a man who desires me, who wants me desperately. Not one who can just as easily live without me." She shrugged sadly. "And judging by how you've reacted to this conversation, I was right. You're not that man."

The whole world had just turned upside down, his blood pounding wildly through his veins.

Jesus, she thought he didn't *want* her?

He lifted a hand, reached for her, not knowing exactly what to say, only knowing he had to tell her she was wrong. *So* wrong.

"Abby, wait, you don't…"

But before he could say another word, the door opened from inside and a trio of giggling teenage girls peered out. Abby took their intrusion as a chance to end the conversation, saying, "Goodbye, Keith," before ducking around them through the door.

Ignoring the girls, he stared after her, frozen into place.

She thought he didn't desire her. Thought he wasn't passionate enough for her. Thought he hadn't had sex with her more than a few times because he wasn't interested…when, in truth, he had to stop himself before he took a lot more than she was ready for.

Even the most basic, vanilla sex he'd had with Abby

had surpassed anything he'd experienced with any-one else. But it had left him so hungry, so desperately aroused, he feared he'd scare the hell out of her with all the wild, sexy things he wanted to do with her. Honor-able, noble heroic types weren't supposed to be that way, right? So he'd stayed away, indulged his need by giving her pleasure, but holding back from his own, until they were married, certain that, deep down, Abby would be every bit as passionate once they were man and wife.

He'd thought he would be teaching a shy pupil the basics, when it appeared she was already ready for the expert class.

He'd misread her, hadn't understood her, hadn't taken the time to find out what she really wanted. When it came to sex, he'd seen only what was on the surface—the lady, the happily-ever-after dreamer. He'd missed seeing the woman.

In short: he'd blown it.

"Idiot," he muttered, mentally calling himself worse names.

But not for long. Soon, the conversation began to take another shape in his mind. His beautiful fiancée had bared her heart, voiced her deepest needs, thinking she was talking to someone who could never fulfill them.

She was wrong. So wrong. And while she had broken their engagement, the woman he loved had also given him hope.

This wasn't over. Not by a long shot. Though she didn't know it, Abby already had exactly the kind of man she wanted.

He just needed to prove it to her.

2

"ABBY? WHERE ARE YOU? Has anyone seen Abby?"

Hearing Bonnie Campbell, one of the other brides-maids, Abby slid lower in the leather chair in which she'd been hiding. Abby wasn't in a partying mood. Or a talking one. So she kept quiet.

After the scene with Keith, Abby had skulked off and found a quiet corner in the library to be alone. Deep in thought, she'd barely registered the murmurs as the reception broke up, people going to their rooms to relax between social events.

She hadn't cried. She'd simply felt…numb.

Her life had changed so drastically. Turned on a dime, or, in her case, on a bridal bouquet. If someone had asked her this morning if she would break her engagement today—to a man she'd been convinced was her one true love—she would have laughed hysterically. Part of her—probably a bigger part than she'd care to admit—was sure she'd made the biggest mistake of her life.

"He didn't try to stop you," she whispered.

No. He hadn't. He'd been stoic and calm, as always, except when she'd talked about their sex life—or lack thereof. Then he'd looked shocked. But that was probably a male ego thing.

It wasn't as if Keith couldn't please her in bed. Far from it. But she wanted someone who was interested in doing it more than once every few months, and who really wanted to participate!

She just didn't understand. Keith was passionate in so many other ways. He worked hard at his job, yet made time to do a lot of pro bono work, and volunteered with a program for at-risk teens. He wasn't a workaholic, he played hard, too—never missing a weekly basketball game with his friends. He even had a creative streak, sometimes picking up the saxophone he'd once thought of playing professionally—before his dream-killing parents had convinced him he was wasting his time.

She *knew* the man was capable of a lot of passion.

Just not with *her*.

"Abby, are you in here?" Reese's sister must have been part bloodhound, because the library doors were suddenly flung wide.

Sighing, Abby peeked over the chair. "I'm here. What is it?"

Bonnie rushed in. "Did you know about the movie people?"

"Yes." Frankly she was grateful for them. When Amanda and Reese had asked for volunteers to go to the other hotel, the Mannings had stepped right up. She doubted they'd be back.

"What are we going to do about it?"

"It's already done," she said as she rose from the seat. "Those who left were fine with moving to the other hotel."

"I'm talking about the bridal suite. Some *Neanderthal* is staying in it," Bonnie snapped, sounding furious.

"I know. But the inn is discounting all the other rooms, and comping tonight's party. Plus, Reese and Amanda can come back and stay in the honeymoon suite anytime, on the house."

"Anytime *except* their wedding night."

In her line of work, snafus were common. This one was a biggie—but the concessions the inn was making had been expensive. And it wasn't like Amanda and Reese required a traditional wedding night—they'd been living together for months.

Abby, on the other hand, might, indeed have had more of a white-sheets event, considering she wasn't far past the virgin state. If she were getting married. Which she wasn't.

I'm not getting married. It still hadn't sunk in.

"This is unacceptable!"

"Amanda and Reese seem to be okay with it."

"Well, I am not okay with it. And I'm going to do something about it." Then, her eyes flashing, Bonnie spun around and left.

Once Bonnie was gone, Abby glanced at the clock. After five. The party would be starting in a few hours, and she needed to get her act together and put on a happy face, for Amanda's benefit.

Tomorrow morning would be soon enough to let everyone know what she'd done. Soon enough to slide the beautiful ring off her left hand and think about a life far different from the one she'd been planning for the past two years.

Soon enough to let herself grieve for the fact that Keith Manning would not be part of that life.

UNLIKE THE RECEPTION, which had been held in the ballroom, the Halloween costume party was taking place in an old barn on the grounds of the inn. As lovely as the mansion had been for the daytime events, the barn was just as perfect for tonight. Unused except for storage, the place was cavernous, with plenty of room for the live band, a bar, a dance floor and dozens of tables.

Though Abby had been looking forward to tonight, now she was in no mood to attend. She couldn't, however, bail on her sister. So, dressed in a slinky Grecian Goddess costume—which she'd chosen because she'd wanted her fiancé to see her as sexy and alluring instead of steady and reliable—she set out across the grounds.

The path between house and barn was lit by an army of glowing jack-o'-lanterns, and the day's rain had left behind a mist that heightened the atmosphere. Fresh bales of hay and scarecrows flanked the sliding barn door. Wood-carved witches flew in silhouette against a cloudy sky broken by beams of watery moonlight. Hand-lettered signs warned visitors to turn back, and threatened danger ahead.

Huh. The only danger Abby would land in tonight would be if her parents came and decided to confront her about her colossal stupidity—at least, that's the term she assumed they would use. Well, one of them, anyway.

Though she'd hoped to evade notice, Abby hadn't even gotten her damp coat off before she was spotted. "There you are," said Amanda, looking radiantly happy. "It's about time."

Seeing her sister's heavy makeup and attire, Abby laughed out loud. No wonder Amanda had kept her costume under wraps. "The Corpse Bride? Seriously?"

Amanda twirled in her tattered gown, sending up puffs of what looked like dust but was probably powder. "Isn't it great?"

For Amanda? "It's perfect. Though I doubt the folks agree."

Amanda shrugged. "They'll never see it. They called, saying this was a young person's thing and they'll come by tomorrow."

Hiding her own relief, Abby looked for any sign of hurt in her sister's face, but saw none. Amanda had moved past years' worth of neglect and disapproval from their parents, living her own life, to hell with the consequences. Abby envied her that. A lot. And today, for the first time, she had to wonder if she was more like her sibling than she'd always believed.

"Now, go. Find that handsome man of yours and have some fun!"

Abby was saved from having to admit Keith wouldn't be here by the arrival of more guests. Slipping away, she headed for an empty table, determined to sit out the party. Accepting a glass of champagne from a passing waiter dressed as a vampire, she settled in a corner, trying to remain unobtrusive.

It didn't work. Because, after congratulating herself on having come in unnoticed by anyone except Amanda, she got that funny, almost indescribable feeling of being watched. Her skin prickled, and a vague sense of awareness had her sitting straighter in the chair. Confused by the unusual sensation, she glanced around to see if someone really *was* staring at her. At first, she noticed nothing—just standard Halloween revelers dressed as fairies, witches and devils, all having a great time.

Then her gaze landed on one partygoer standing near the bar, and stopped dead.

Abby sucked in a quick, surprised breath. Not because the man in black was staring at her—he wasn't—but because of his costume. He was literally, the Man in

Black. The Dread Pirate Roberts, aka Westley, from her *favorite* movie of all time, *The Princess Bride*.

Her heart fluttered a little, as it had the first time she'd seen the movie as a closeted-romantic teenager. She'd loved the story, the romance, the "perfect" kiss, the grandeur, the excitement, the happily-ever-after. Most of all, she'd loved the mysterious man-in-black—an ultimate Prince Charming who'd literally climbed mountains and fought giants for the one he loved. And now, for the first time in her life, she was seeing him in person. Well, sort of.

"Hot, isn't he?" someone murmured.

Abby glanced up to see Jazz, her sister's best friend. The maid of honor looked incredibly uncomfortable in a fluffy, frilly blue ball gown with big, hoop skirts. Nobody would ever mistake Jazz Wilkes for Cinderella, but somehow, she still managed to look absolutely stunning in a costume that she clearly disliked.

"Beyond hot," she agreed, seeing the other woman's eyes locked on the stranger, too.

"The Spanish guy was always my favorite in that movie, but this dude definitely has me reconsidering."

Completely understandable. With the billowing, lace-front pirate shirt, tight black pants, knee-high boots, gloves, the scarf and mask covering most of his face, he had totally nailed the costume. But the most breath-stopping part was that he wore the clothes like they'd been made just for him—like he *was* the character. The outfit fit his incredible body to a T, showcasing the rock-solid form. He was lean, broad-shouldered, slim-hipped. The pants verged on indecent and she, the "good girl," cast a few discreet glances there. Frankly there was a lot to look at. A whole lot.

As if that weren't enough, he also had an incredibly

sensuous mouth, which was emphasized by the mask that covered everything down to his nose. Eminently kissable.

Utterly dazzling.

"Wonder where Buttercup's hiding," Jazz mused. "I bet I could take her."

"I'm quite sure you could. Still, she's probably around here somewhere," Abby said with a smile. Jazz was definitely a ballsy one. "I can't see a guy coming in *that* without a girlfriend having forced it on him."

"Or the bride," Jazz grumbled, carelessly fluffing her own dress, with its layers of blue satin and white netting.

Suddenly Jazz whistled. "Stick out your chest, he's coming over!"

The other woman was right. The stranger was weaving through the crowd, skirting the dance floor, headed this way. Abby turned and quickly looked around— definitely *not* sticking out her chest—wondering if his missing princess bride was sitting nearby.

It honestly didn't occur to her that he was heading for her table until he stopped right beside it.

"Dance?"

His voice was mysterious—a whisper, low, throaty, supersexy. The one-word invitation was as much a command as a request, and Abby quivered a little in her seat, wondering why Jazz hadn't yet dragged the guy out onto the dance floor.

When the maid of honor nudged her not-so-gently in the shoulder, she realized the man *hadn't* been talking to Jazz.

"Me?" she squeaked.

His dark eyes glittering behind the mask as he stared down at her, he nodded.

Abby's heart was racing; she hadn't come here to dance or actually have a good time. She'd broken her engagement less than six hours ago for heaven's sake. This man couldn't know that, obviously, but she still wore a big rock on her left hand, and it hadn't deterred him one bit.

"Come on."

No. No way was she ready to get next to another man—even one who seemed to have stepped out of her deepest fantasies. She instinctively shook her head. "No, thanks."

"Pull up your big girl panties and go dance with the man," Jazz snapped, nudging her again, this time harder.

"I'm sorry…"

"Please," he urged, extending a gloved hand.

Abby looked at it, then up at him, then at Jazz—who was more attractive. Drop-dead gorgeous, in fact. Why this incredibly sexy stranger would have chosen *her*, she simply didn't know.

One thing she did know—he wasn't going to *let* her refuse. Without another word, he lifted her hand into his and tugged her to her feet. She allowed it, helpless to do anything but follow—silent, breathless—as he led her into the crowd of dancers.

The band had been playing standard Halloween stuff—the "Time Warp," the "Monster Mash." But suddenly, as the man in black stopped walking and turned to face her for the dance, the music segued into something slow. A torchy old blues song about black magic.

Black magic. Yes, that fit. Because it was as if he'd cast a spell on her, pulling every lucid thought from her brain and every word of refusal from her tongue. She couldn't think, couldn't speak. And when he stepped close, she was sure her heart would stop dead in her chest.

"Okay?" he whispered, the word riding a warm exhalation.

"Um..."

"Relax." He laced their fingers together, then twisted his arm around hers, bent both of them, and lifted their clenched hands between their chests. It wasn't a standard dance position, but rather intimate. Personal. Familiar.

The way they stood also put the side of his silk-covered arm against the outer curve of her breast. Abby trembled, shocked to her core by the waves of excitement rolling through her.

Beneath her flowing white gown, her breasts tightened. Not abundantly curved, she didn't always wear a bra, and the cut of this costume made it difficult. So the only thing separating her sensitive skin from his hard, hot chest were two silky layers of fabric—her dress, and his shirt. The material didn't offer protection, merely heightened the extreme intimacy of their embrace, bringing erotic whispers of sensation to her nipples.

He made a sound—something like a groan, and she knew he was aware of it, that he could feel the pebbled tips of her breasts brushing against him. Embarrassed, she considered pulling away, leaving the party before this got too crazy. But something stopped her. Her own instincts? Or the certainty that he wouldn't let her go? Both?

As if knowing she wanted to flee, he slid his other arm possessively around her waist, a big, strong hand flattening against the small of her back. The tips of the stranger's fingers rested so close to the curves of her bottom, she instinctively jerked away. Which meant she arched *toward* something else: his groin. Her reactive movement had slammed their already close hips into a hot, wanton connection.

She gasped. Tried to pull back.

He kept her still, not letting her ease away. Not seeming to care that his hips ground into hers, that she could feel his hot, male sex pressing into the juncture of her thighs—and getting bigger by the second.

Good Lord.

If not for their clothes, they could be having sex, right here on the dance floor surrounded by other people. There was absolutely no way he would be able to hide his physical reaction if she was to walk away. And he didn't seem to give a damn.

"You're beautiful," he whispered.

She shook her head.

"I mean it. You're the most beautiful woman here."

"I think your vision's been impaired—either that or your mask has slipped down too far over your eyes."

"Do you always react to those kinds of compliments with sarcasm?"

"Do you always offer those kinds of compliments to complete strangers?"

"What can I say? You're just so damn sexy, I can't help myself. I can't stop thinking about those big girl panties."

Abby swallowed hard, shocked at the intimacies in his voice. An image flashed through her mind—this man, lifting her dress, inch by inch, making his way toward the so-not-for-little-girls thong she wore underneath.

"I can't take my eyes off you."

"You don't even know me," she said, confused, on edge, knowing something crazy was going on and not sure why she didn't much care. Her heart was racing,

her breaths shallow and raspy and all she could think
was— *What is happening to me?*

Though he had been speaking in a low whisper, they
were still surrounded by people, and somebody dancing too close could probably overhear them. Still, she
remained in his arms, not wanting the strange interlude
to end just yet.

"I mean it. I want you so badly I can barely stand up
straight."

She tried to pull away. Again, he wouldn't give her
as much as an inch.

"Breathe," he ordered.

"I don't think I can."

He moved his face closer, until his scarf-covered
cheek brushed hers, and every inch of their bodies
touched, from face to calf. Holding her breath, Abby
melted against him, sure of absolutely nothing except
this felt so good, she couldn't resist. Slowly they began
to sway, moving to the music, each tilt of their bodies
giving a little, taking a little, building the tension yet
also feeling so incredibly right.

Finally she relaxed enough to do as he'd ordered, and
breathed deeply. His warm, masculine scent filled her
nostrils, and sense memory finally filled in the rest, answering all the questions. Somehow, she couldn't muster
surprise as she acknowledged the truth. The costume
had thrown her for a few minutes, since it was *so* out of
character, so unexpected. As was the incredibly sexy,
suggestive conversation.

But oh, yes, she knew him.

She knew that scent. She knew the voice hidden behind the raspy whisper. She knew that body. She knew the sensations he was bringing forth in her.

The only thing she didn't know was what Keith Manning—her ex-fiancé—was up to.

3

KEITH'S INTENTION hadn't been to trick Abby. He hadn't worn the costume to try to disguise himself, or changed his voice with the intention of seducing her as a stranger. No. The whole point of tonight was to show her that he, Keith Manning, was absolutely the man she wanted. He didn't want to entice her to cheat…not even if she did it with *him!*

But he'd also known getting her into his arms, on the dance floor—getting her to *listen*—wouldn't be easy if he showed up in the costume she'd chosen for him. She'd take one look at him and put her guard up. Her emotions were still tangled, she'd be defensive and wary.

Besides, it wasn't something he could tell her. He needed to show her, prove the point, make the grand gesture. She deserved it.

Hence his costume: the Man in Black. He had decided to become the idealized, romanticized hero from the movie she so loved. And now he had her right where he wanted her, right where she belonged. In his arms.

He felt the moment she fully relaxed, and suspected she'd finally figured out who she was dancing with. But he wasn't sure, not entirely. So he couldn't give up the game just yet.

"Better now?"

"Better. I like your costume," she whispered.

"I like yours, too."

"I take it there's no Buttercup lurking around?"

"Who's that?"

"The Man in Black's true love." She huffed a little. "Have you never paid attention to the movie?"

He couldn't help chuckling. The only thing he remembered about the movie was that Abby loved it, and there was a dude dressed all in black who was damned good with a sword.

"How on earth did you get it so quickly?"

Ah. Confirmation. She definitely knew. "A client of mine is married to the director of a theater company in Chicago. I called, she had something she thought would work, so I went and picked it up."

She nibbled her bottom lip. "You drove all the way to Chicago and back just to get a costume?"

He nodded.

"Why? If you wanted to come to the party, you could have worn the one I got you."

"Let's just say I wanted to find something I knew would get your attention," he admitted.

"It definitely worked. You got it."

"Good."

They were silent for a moment, swaying a little, then she said, "I do like this one better than the one I bought."

"Yeah, I know. But I could never figure out why. This character wasn't the Prince Charming you told me you always wanted."

"When I was twelve," she said with a chuckle.

Keith sighed, wondering how he could be considered smart when he'd been so utterly stupid about this woman.

"Besides, the prince was a creep in that movie," she told him. "Westley was much more exciting."

"You like that he was a mystery man, then?"

She shook her head slowly, tilting it back to look up at him. Her brown eyes were wide as she studied his face, her gaze resting long on his mouth, as if she were thinking what it would be like to kiss a masked man—even one she'd kissed a thousand times before.

"Not necessarily," she finally replied.

"Swordsman?"

"Not that, either."

"Pirate?"

At last she laughed softly. "No." Though she probably didn't know it, she pressed against him even harder, relaxed and so naturally seductive every one of his senses went into hyperdrive. "Well, okay, maybe a little. Pirates are very sexy these days. I think I was ahead of the trend on that one, having such a mad crush on you...er, I mean, on that character."

"But he wasn't all pirate," he added, trying to remember more of the details from the film, which Abby watched at least once every year—and had suckered him into watching once, too.

"No, he wasn't. There was a very tender, but passionate lover underneath all that black."

Passionate. She'd said that earlier, that she wanted passion. He'd had it to spare, he'd just never trusted himself—or their relationship—enough to share it with her.

Well, that was done. Finished. He knew some of what she wanted, and intended to find out the rest. Then he would go about giving it to her for all the days of their lives, if she'd only let him.

"Passionate, huh?" he asked. "How do you know? I think that film was rated PG at most."

"I had to use my imagination." She licked her lips, staring up at him, her expression so guileless, he was caught totally unprepared when she added, "Though, I would have preferred some graphic, X-rated scenes."

Keith paused midstep, letting his mind wrap around that. Abby—kind, friendly, sweet-natured, inexperienced Abby—fantasized about watching porn? God, how much did he not know about this woman he'd planned to marry?

"You like to watch other people have sex?" he asked, the words almost choking him.

"I don't know. Maybe. There's so much I haven't done, I don't know what I'd like."

"That's a crime against nature," he growled.

"Not knowing what I'd like?"

"Never having the chance to find out." He brushed his lips against her ear, hearing her sigh at the contact. "Why don't you tell me what you want to try, in your quest to find out what you might like?"

She hesitated. "I'm not used to talking about things like that."

"Another crime against nature," he admitted, mentally kicking himself all over again. "Please, Abby," he added, "please talk to me. Give me a chance."

"A chance to do what?"

He answered with his heart. "To save us."

"It's…"

"Don't say it's too late," he ordered. "Don't say everything went wrong without at least giving me a chance to show you why you and I are so right."

She stared up at him, searchingly, as if trying to see the real man behind the mask. Hell, maybe she'd never seen him. Maybe he'd never *let* her see him.

He knew he'd never let her see the man who'd wanted her so desperately. "Please," he urged. "Open up. Share your fantasies with me. Tell me what you want. You can trust me."

There could be no more hesitation, no more holding back. Abby did trust him, in every other way, he knew that. Now he was asking her to take a gamble and trust him with her most erotic longings.

Her eyes drifted closed. She fell silent. Then, maybe it was the mask, or the music, or the plea in his voice or the fact that she'd dumped his ass today, something made her open up about things they'd never discussed. Her voice sounding almost dreamy, she said, "I want everything. Just everything."

He wanted to know more. He needed to know more.

"Specifics."

She hesitated for a second. Licking her lips, she admitted, "I want to be tied up."

Holy shit. He missed a step in the dance and almost landed a boot-clad foot on her toes.

"I'm not into serious bondage or S&M—at least, I don't think I am…."

Thank God for that.

"But I think I could like being gently restrained, unable to do anything except feel every sensation and accept every bit of intimacy I can get."

Keith's teeth clenched and he hissed each breath between them. The woman was killing him here. Absolutely killing him.

"I see," he finally mumbled. "Go on."

She did, without any hesitation, as if now that she'd opened the floodgates, she couldn't hold back against the current of her feelings. "I want to have sex in a public place, where there's a risk of exposure."

He almost tripped again. Exhibitionism. Abby. Unreal. "Anyplace in particular?"

"It doesn't matter. The fear of discovery is the key part."

Catching the vision himself, he said, "During a game at Wrigley."

She let out a sound like a purr, deep in her beautiful throat. "In the backseat of your car while it's parked at the stadium."

"I'm liking this idea," he told her. "And I also liked the first one. So far, we're two for two."

"I also want…"

A couple dressed as Fred and Wilma Flintstone danced a little too close, and she snapped her mouth closed. He suspected that whatever she'd been about to say, it was very naughty.

He could hardly wait. Drawing her closer to the edge of the floor, as far away from the cave-couple as he could get, he said, "Go on. What else?"

Her voice low, she replied, "I want oral sex to be only foreplay—an appetizer rather than an entire meal."

Wow. Direct hit. That hadn't just been a fantasy, it had been an accusation, aimed right at him. And he couldn't deny that it stung. "I thought you liked…"

"I do like it," she insisted, nodding as she stared into his eyes. "I love it. I love getting it, but I'd like to be on the giving side, too." Her throat quivered as she swallowed and her voice fell to a sultry whisper. "I'd also love to both give and get at the same time."

"God," he muttered, his mind flooding with those

images. The idea of Abby's perfect mouth wrapped around his cock as he licked her into insanity almost had him exploding in his stupid pirate pants. "I never thought you'd be into that."

"You never asked."

"My mistake. And believe me, I regret it." He definitely did, especially now when those images continued to play in full Technicolor glory in his brain. Not to mention engorging his cock.

"The point is," she told him, "it needs to be about arousing each other till we're out of our minds. Then we have sex." She sounded earnest. Serious. "I might come, but I'm still left almost desperate with wanting you inside me."

She thought he didn't feel the same way. Thought he hadn't felt like his heart would rupture every time he'd pleasured her and then walked away to a lonely shower and a tight fist.

"I want sweet sex, like we've had, Keith. It's been wonderful. But I also want it wild and hot and intense."

"Again, I didn't know," he whispered.

"Would it have mattered if you did?"

"Of course!"

She shrugged, looking almost helpless and her eyes were moist. "Well, I didn't know if you were even interested, if you were holding back, if you had to force yourself to do as much as you did, if there was someone else…"

"No. Not once. Not ever."

She nodded in acknowledgment of that. "Okay. Still, I'm just telling you what I've been thinking. I never *knew* and I was so damned frustrated. I actually had to buy myself a battery-operated boyfriend and read the hottest romance novels I could find just to get some relief, and it still wasn't enough. Because I wanted *you*."

He closed his eyes, both incredibly turned on, but also feeling like utter shit for having left her so desperate.

"I'm sorry." Keith was barely moving, not even really pretending to dance anymore. Neither was Abby. She seemed completely intent on her every word. All around them the dancers continued; the music changed, the tempo sped up, but they slowed, and slowed, until they were utterly still. "You can't imagine how sorry, Abs."

"Let me put it bluntly."

"You mean you haven't been so far?" he asked, still mystified and shocked at the way they'd been at such cross-purposes, both wanting the same thing, neither opening up enough to admit it. And his head continued to swim with incredibly vivid sexual images—all the things he'd wanted to do with her for so long... She'd wanted them, too.

She didn't laugh. "The truth is, I like being who I am in public, and I can even stand to have a man who won't flirt with me or give me deep, wet French kisses when anybody else is around."

Yeah. That'd be him. Though, not for the reasons she might think.

"But in private, in my bed, I want to be someone's sexual obsession." She pressed her lips into the nape of his neck, licking, nipping a little. "I want sex that lasts for hour after hour, in all kinds of positions. Sex that feels so good it's almost painful. Rough and sweaty and intense and possibly illegal in some states."

He let out a sound, half laugh, half groan, so incredibly turned on he didn't know if he'd be able to remain on his feet for much longer.

"I want it in every way it's possible for a man and a woman to have it," she said. "And then I want it all again."

He nodded, unable to speak.

"Most of all," she said, "I want the man I'm with to be just as desperate for all those things as I am. To want me with every ounce of his being."

"I do," he said, the words torn from deep inside him, an admission he'd been holding back for far too long. "I swear to you, I do."

She shook her head sadly. "How could a man who wanted me that much be able to strip my clothes off and give me pleasure and then just walk out the door?"

"Like checking an orgasm off a to-do list?" he asked, remembering what she'd said earlier.

"Yes."

"Only a very stupid man who couldn't see what was right in front of him would do that." He lifted a hand to the back of her head, twining his fingers in her silky brown hair that she'd curled into long, goddesslike ringlets. Tugging it slightly so she had to tilt her head and look up at him, he admitted in a hoarse voice, "You and I have got a lot to talk about. A lot to clear up."

He bent down and brushed his lips across hers, sliding his tongue between them, sharing a breath, a heartbeat, a silent promise.

"I thought we were talking," she whispered against his mouth.

"It's a start. But there are some things you need to know. And I intend to tell you. Only, right now, Abs, if I don't get you alone somewhere and fuck you until neither one of us can move, I'm going to embarrass myself right here in the middle of your sister's party."

ABBY'S HEART WAS POUNDING so hard, it was a wonder she could remain standing. Her legs had grown as weak as sticks of warm butter and her sex throbbed with sheer desire. She was desperate for him. Inflamed. Their sexy conversation about what she wanted was wild enough— she'd just never imagined what a turn-on raw, graphic language could be. Keith had never spoken to her like that. Nobody had. And right now, at this moment, she was more excited than she had ever been in her entire life.

He was obviously in the same boat, at least judging by the huge erection pressed against her groin. Getting out of here with *that* would be a trick.

"Follow me," she said, pulling away and spinning around so her back was toward him. They were at the edge of the dance floor, unnoticed by most of the other partygoers, who were all gyrating and laughing. Apparently nobody had noticed the erotic-romance-novel-worthy moment taking place a few feet away.

That's how she felt. Like the sexually charged heroine of one of those novels she so loved to read. She would never have dreamed of saying such intimate, sexual things a few years ago. Now, she was different…no longer unsure of who she was, or how she would act. No longer determined to play the good girl role just because her big sister had the bad one all sewn up.

She wasn't good. She wasn't bad. She was just a woman who finally had the guts to admit what she really wanted.

Like one of those heroines in the books, she knew just what to do to get it. Reaching for one of his hands, she tugged him after her and headed not for the big sliding door at the front, through which she'd entered—it was way too crowded over there and they'd have to say good-night. Instead she went the other way.

She'd toured this place a few months back, when planning the party, and remembered the layout. From this big, open area, a dark hallway extended back through a maze of long-unused stalls. At the end was an office... and another exit that would put them within twenty feet of the inn.

And her room. And her bed.

"Where are we going?"

"Back way out," she told him, speaking over her shoulder. She couldn't turn around and look at him, couldn't see the raw hunger in his face, not if she wanted to stay focused on moving forward until they could get somewhere private.

Within a dozen strides, they were out of the well-lit party area, disappearing into the back half of the barn. They had no sooner been swallowed by the shadows when Keith stopped her.

"I have to touch you," he muttered. "Please." Moving closer behind her, he slipped an arm around her waist and pulled her back against him. Abby sighed, awash with pleasure as he moved his warm mouth to her neck. Kissing, biting lightly, he whispered more of those crazy-erotic words, telling her what he intended to do to her.

Wild things. Wicked things. Dangerous things. Things she'd dreamed and fantasized about doing with him but had never thought would actually happen.

Her already damp sex grew slick and swollen against her tiny panties. Unable to help it, she had to grind back against him, desperate for some relief. That thick ridge pressed hard against her, and she writhed, feeling the silk-encased heat edge between the curves of her bottom.

Keith continued exploring her neck and the vulnerable spot at its nape, nipping, sucking, kissing. She was whimpering by the time his hand dropped down to the juncture of her thighs. Cupping her, he pulled her more firmly against him, using his fingers to toy with her sex while his member nestled ever tighter against her backside.

The position was wicked. Hinted at all kinds of wild sexual things they could do, and the ways in which they could do them.

Abby wanted to try them all.

"I want you like this," he growled, as if reading her thoughts. "Want to lift you up and slide you down on me, just…like…*this*."

"Yes, yes." The idea of being taken from behind, or while standing up, or *anything* other than basic man-on-top excited her beyond belief.

Lifting his other hand, he pushed the strap of her dress—a filmy strip of fabric—off her shoulder and let it fall, baring her breast to the cool night air. He stroked her, toyed with her nipple—tweaking, pinching lightly—until she felt a moan rise up in her throat.

They were no more than twenty feet from the crowd. Lost in shadows, but still easily visible should anyone venture down this way. Keith was already fulfilling one of her fantasies.

It was dangerous. And incredibly erotic. And pretty dumb. This wasn't a baseball field where they'd be anonymous—her sister's big new family, and a lot of friends, were the ones who would catch them if they got any crazier.

Yes, she was dying to continue. But letting this go

any further would just make it more painful when they finally did stop to get somewhere more private. "Come on, we should get out of here before I refuse to let you stop."

He stepped back, let her shift her dress back into place, then took her hand again as they headed for the exit. Their footsteps clicked on the floor, creating a rapid tattoo that matched her heartbeat, their anxiousness and desperation audible and thick as the night itself.

When they reached the door, Keith threw his arm out, prepared to open it without even slowing down.

Suddenly realizing something, though, Abby grabbed his hand and stopped him. "Don't!" Shaking in utter disappointment, she pointed to the red Emergency sign. The door was equipped with an alarm. If they went through it, everybody back at the party would be forced to leave to make sure there was no fire, or else come investigate.

"You've gotta be kidding me," Keith groaned.

"I know." Frustration made her whole body quiver as she imagined having to go back into the party, back through the crowd, smiling, making small-talk, saying good-night, hiding the fact that she was dripping wet and so aroused she thought she might die if she didn't get him inside her soon. "I can't..."

"Neither can I," he snapped.

And then her sexy ex-fiancé—God, had she really jilted this man, thinking he wasn't *passionate?*—lifted her into his arms and strode toward the nearest abandoned stall. He kicked open the swinging door with one booted foot and carried her inside.

The place had been converted years ago, the floor was bare, the air a bit musty with disuse. But it was dark. And semiprivate. "Good enough," she said.

He didn't reply. Instead he was already grabbing the sleeves of her dress and pushing them down, tearing the fabric, not that she cared. The dress fell in a wispy heap, puddling around her high-heel-clad feet, leaving her wearing nothing but a lacy thong.

They both completely ignored the party going on in the front of the building, though the music and voices were audible from back here. They could be discovered by anyone who decided to do some exploring. It wasn't like the swinging stall door actually gave them any real privacy.

I don't care. I so don't care.

"You are the sexiest thing I have ever seen," he muttered, devouring her with a long, desperate stare. Keith looked like a man trying to decide which dish to try first at a banquet table. "Did you really think I didn't want you?"

"You gave a pretty good impression of it."

"I'm sorry, Abby. You can't imagine how sorry," he said, pressing a warm kiss on her lips. Their tongues slid together, tasting deeply. Each breath was shared; even their heartbeats seemed to fall into sync.

They'd kissed a thousand times. And at first, this kiss held a hint of that same gentleness. But it soon changed as pure, unbridled lust took over. They devoured each other's mouths—she wanted to memorize the taste of him, the scrape of his teeth, the slide of his tongue.

When the kiss finally ended, Keith immediately dropped to his knees, pressing his mouth into her middle and breathing her in like he could imprint her very essence onto his lungs. She reached for the mask and scarf, tugging them off and tossing them away, revealing his handsome face striped with shadow. The desperate desire she saw there was enough to stop her heart.

It was true. This man was dying for her. Keith Manning wanted her beyond all rational thought. Just as she'd always hoped he would. He was her dream man again, the one she'd wanted, the one she loved. The one she'd intended to marry.

What had changed, she didn't know. If she'd misread him, missed the signals, just been too inexperienced to understand…well, that was all in the past. Now there was only this. This gorgeous, sexy, amazing man—the man she loved—on his knees. Loving her. *Wanting* her.

As she wanted him. Not just now…always.

She hadn't yet taken off the ring. She only hoped he didn't want her to.

Twining her fingers in his thick, dark hair, she watched as Keith pressed hot, openmouthed kisses on her stomach, then slowly rose to explore her breasts. He covered one taut tip, sucking hard—deep and shocking—then went to the other. The night was cold against her damp skin and her nipples tightened even more. Sensation flooded her—the air against her body, his spicy masculine scent heady and intoxicating, his mouth doing such incredible things to her breast, his hands warm and heavy against her hips.

"This! I've wanted this for so long," she whispered, almost wonderingly.

"Not as long as I have," he said, kissing his way back down her body. This time, he didn't stop at her stomach. He tasted her hip, then lower, to the hollow just above her pelvic bone. His lips tracing the line where the thin stripe of elastic rode above the small thatch of curls covering her sex. Sweeping the thong off with a scrape of one fingertip, he bared her for a more intimate caress.

This time, when he licked and nibbled her sensitive clit—bringing a yelp of pure satisfaction to her mouth—Abby didn't wonder if the amazing oral sex would be the end of their evening. Tonight, she knew, it would be only the beginning.

Almost as if the knowledge of that was enough to inspire it, an orgasm washed over her, sudden, hot, intense. Crying out, she sobbed his name. Her hips jerked, and he squeezed his hands around them, his fingers digging into her backside as he continued devouring her as she came against his mouth.

"Appetizer," he muttered against her when she'd finally stopped shaking.

"Yeah."

He rose quickly, as if knowing her patience for slow, sweet caresses was absolutely gone. She wanted power. Desperation.

Possession.

Reaching for his shirt, she didn't waste time with buttons. Instead she tugged it up and helped him yank it over his head. He tossed it on the ground, then went for the waistband of his pants. Abby stroked his chest, rubbing the tips of her fingers across the long ridges of muscle, twining them in the crisp hair.

He unfastened the pants and shoved them down his hips. Neither of them could wait long enough for him to get them all the way off. She simply reached for him, wrapping her hand around the rock-hard shaft, so desperate she knew she would beg if she had to.

"Abby," he groaned, thrusting into her hand. "I've got to be in you."

"Do it!"

Pressing her back into a corner, he grabbed one of her thighs and lifted it over his hip. Abby arched toward him, gasping when he thrust into her, hard and deep.

This was no slow, quiet lovemaking. It was everything

she'd told him she wanted. And far better than she'd ever dreamed.

They remained very still for a moment, and Abby savored his powerful intrusion into her body. She squeezed him, deep inside, and felt him shudder in response.

Buried to the hilt, Keith pressed his face in her hair and breathed deeply. "Okay?"

She twined her arms around his shoulders, digging her nails lightly into his muscles. "More than."

"Hold on."

She held on.

Reaching for her other thigh, Keith picked her up and wrapped both her legs around his waist, cupping her bottom in his big, strong hands to support her weight. He drew out, then thrust again. Harder. Faster. Each time digging a little deeper, carving out more of a place for himself inside her. She felt like he was claiming her as his own, planting his flag.

His breathing grew more rapid, as did hers. Keith pressed her back against the wall; the wood planks dug into her skin, but she barely noticed it. All she could feel was the fullness, the pounding of all that heat against her womb, his mouth on her neck, his heart beating against hers.

All she could feel was absolutely glorious.

And most of all, *wanted*.

4

HE'D RIPPED HER DRESS.

Not just ripped it, he'd torn the thing beyond repair.

Funny, though, Abby didn't seem to mind one bit. In fact, the look on her face was pure feminine satisfaction, as if she loved the fact that she'd driven him to such lengths.

Hell, she *did* love it. Every word she'd said to him today proved that much.

She just hadn't anticipated that he'd love it even more.

God, they had been running in circles around each other for so long, it was no wonder they'd almost lost what they had. If he hadn't had the sense to come here tonight—to show her how much he desired her and what he'd do for her—they likely really would have remained apart. He'd have gone back to Chicago and buried himself in work to get over her, to bury the pain. And Abby would have done the same. Both always wondering, neither reaching for the phone.

They'd come close…so close. He never wanted to be that close to losing everything he'd ever wanted again. Which meant he'd do whatever he had to to make sure she never doubted his feelings—and his desire—for her again.

He'd shown her the truth—taken her the way he'd always wanted to. Now it was time to talk to the woman… to let her know tonight wasn't a fluke. Abby needed to understand that he'd felt this way about her since the first time he'd set eyes on her.

But not here, not in a stall. Not when anybody could walk back here and spy her with her dress torn to shreds—and his back equally shredded by her sharp nails.

"Maybe if I tie it like a halter?" she mumbled, trying to shimmy her costume around and use two undamaged straps to tie around her neck.

"Sorry, beautiful, you still look like somebody ripped your clothes off and ravaged you."

"Mmm. Ravaged. By the Dread Pirate Roberts."

Keith laughed, pressing another kiss against her lips. "Or the Dread Lawyer Manning."

She giggled, so adorably sweet and so irresistibly hot he wanted to have her all over again.

Soon. Conversation first.

"Uh, why don't you just tie it around your waist and put my shirt on. You can say you spilled something on yourself.

"So I get to look like a klutz rather than a sex goddess?"

He lifted a hand to her cheek, scraping the side of his thumb across her lips. "You *are* my sex goddess, Abs."

"Well, it's about time you worshipped at my altar, then," she quipped, raising a brow in challenge.

"Yeah. It is. Now let's get out of here and find a

private place so I can make another sacrifice to your sexiness."

"What are you going to sacrifice this time?"

"I dunno," he said, wagging his brows, "you definitely drew blood on my back. What more do you want?"

Gasping, she bit her lip. "I'm so sorry."

"I'm not. Now, let's get out of here. I think it's time for our talk."

"I'm all ears."

He glanced down at her naked body. "Actually you're all breasts right now, at least as far as I can see. And while I'm not complaining, I would hate to have to stop on the way out of here to beat the crap out of some guy who got to see you like this, too. So let me grab that shirt for you."

"Yeah, right. So you can walk through the party with that gorgeous body half-naked and my claw marks on your back? Then I'd be the one beating somebody up."

"The scratches would show I'm taken," he pointed out. "Very thoroughly."

She playfully smacked his upper arm. "I have a better idea. I left my coat draped over the back of my chair. If you go get it, I'll just put it on and button it up. Nobody will ever know what I'm wearing—or not wearing— underneath. And that way I won't have to scratch out another woman's eyes for ogling you in all your bare-chested glory."

She sounded a tiny bit jealous, something he'd never heard from her before. He liked it. He liked everything about this new Abby…on top of loving her with all his heart.

"Okay, wait here," he said, kissing her one more time, then donning his shirt. He didn't bother tucking it in, or putting the mask back on. The party was in full swing—loud, with lots of champagne and beer being consumed. He doubted anybody would even notice him.

A dress-ripped-off-her Abby? Yes. But not a slightly disheveled pirate.

When he reached the party, he blinked a few times to allow his eyes to adjust to the bright light. Then he made his way through the crowd, trying to remember which table Abby had been sitting at. It took a couple of minutes, and when he finally did locate it, he realized someone else had taken a seat in the chair.

He blinked again. Because that looked a whole lot like Drew Ericson, an actor who'd made his name synonymous with shoot-'em-up-action-flicks. "Excuse me," he said. "Do you mind…"

"Yes. He minds," someone interjected with a sigh. "He's a guest of honor and I've been ordered by the bride and groom to babysit him and make sure he has a good time. So, sorry, no autographs."

That, surprisingly, came from one of the other bridesmaids. The one with curly hair—the groom's sister, he believed. He'd first thought she was a quiet little thing, but she sounded pretty annoyed now. Ericson rolled his eyes and shrugged good-naturedly, seemingly amused by his "babysitter."

"Actually I just need to get the coat he's sitting on," Keith said. "It's Abby's."

The actor immediately rose. "Sorry, man."

"Oh, I'm so sorry, too," said the bridesmaid, flushing a little. "It's been a…strange day."

Keith couldn't help smiling, thinking his had been absolutely fantastic. "Hope it gets better for you," he said, grabbing the coat. Then he headed back for the hallway, skirting the wall so he wouldn't be too obvious when he turned down it. Fortunately he wasn't spotted, and got back to a pacing Abby no more than five minutes after he'd left.

"You found it?"

"Underneath a movie star, no less."

Her eyes widened.

"Doesn't matter," he said, helping her slip the coat on. He carefully buttoned it, then stepped back to inspect her.

"Do I look okay?"

Other than the fact that her thick, beautiful hair had fallen out of its curls and hung in sexy disarray around her face, her lips were swollen and red, she had a few abrasions on her neck from his roughened cheek, and her eyes were sparkling with secretive pleasure?

"You look like someone who's just been thoroughly shagged."

She laughed. "Well, then, let's hope nobody looks too closely."

Nobody did, and within ten minutes, they had made their escape from the party and headed across the grounds to the inn. The full moon above had brightened, the day's rain clouds having finally drifted away. Dried leaves crunched beneath their feet and the air smelled wet and earthy. They didn't usually experience nights like this in the city, and he found himself liking it a lot.

Abby seemed to, as well. Because instead of heading toward the front door, she suddenly veered right, tugging him along with her. Further down the lawn stood a pretty gazebo, and he realized right away that was where she was headed.

"Is this okay?" she asked as she stepped up into it.

"Very."

They sat down on a bench, and for the longest time, said nothing, merely soaking up the evening. And thinking about what would happen now. Then Abby made a tiny sound, like a throat-clearing, that told him she was ready to talk. Turning to look at her, he saw the way she bit the corner of her lip. She appeared tight and tense, averting her gaze, and, the biggest tell of all, twisted the ring on her left hand.

"Don't," he ordered, knowing exactly what she was about to say.

"Don't what?"

"Don't kick yourself for dumping my sorry ass."

"I didn't really…"

"Yeah, babe. You did."

She turned her stricken face toward him, staring him in the eye. "I am so sorry."

Keith slid an arm across her shoulder. "I'm the one who's sorry. I wasn't honest with you. Or with myself. You had every reason to doubt me and more reason to bail out." He gently kissed her temple. "The thing is, I was operating under this delusion that you were too good."

"Too good for you? That's ridiculous."

He shook his head. Then, wanting her in his arms, he pulled her off the bench and into his lap, taking one of her hands in his, the other resting on the small of her back.

"Actually I thought you were too good, too pure, for the kind of sex I wanted to have with you."

Her jaw dropped open. "You wanna repeat that?"

He sighed heavily. "I guess it sounds crazy. Maybe it was. I had this whole idea of how a man is supposed to act around his fiancée—or his wife. What he should do, and what he shouldn't. I wanted you like crazy. God,

Abby, I took so many cold showers and jerked-off so often it's a wonder I didn't break my dick."

She couldn't hide a smile, obviously liking that he'd been so desperate.

"But the things I fantasized about *doing* with you—to you—just didn't seem like the kinds of thoughts I should be having about the woman I wanted to marry. The one who would bear my children." He frowned. "The one who seemed so romantic, so sure of the possibility of Prince Charming and happily-ever-after. I wanted to be that for you, Abby. Wanted you to see that white knight I sense you've been looking for since you were a little kid being raised in a cold, loveless house."

Tears rose in her eyes and he suspected he'd hit the nail on the head with that one. It wasn't hard to see why Abby had held on to those fantasies, especially once her sister had left and she'd been alone in the mausoleum, hoping for a way out, too used to being the good daughter to dream of breaking free for herself.

"You were," she told him. "Honestly, you were. I just realized very early on that I wanted the real man, not the noble prince."

"You've got him," he told her. "I know you didn't before—I never let on, never let you see. I treated you like…well, like a goddess. But a stone one, not a warm, flesh and blood one."

She reached up and unbuttoned her coat, then drew his hand to her chest, whispering, "I'm warm, flesh and blood."

He bent down and brushed his mouth across the top curve of her lovely breast, above her steadily beating heart. "I know. I'm sorry I put you on a pedestal."

She nodded, accepting his apology. "Let me guess… leaving aside the idea that you had to be some noble being in order to deserve me, and that my view of love and relationships came from one too many fairy tales, *yours* came from your parents?"

Shifting uncomfortably, he admitted to both of them, "Probably."

"I have to be honest," she said, a frown tugging at her brow. "I don't really like your parents. But if it helps, I don't like mine very much, either. Love them. But don't like them."

He laughed, delighted by her honesty, her openness. Abby had always been warm and funny, at least when she wasn't around her family or others who had certain expectations of her. Now, though, with all the barriers down, he really liked the way she wasn't pulling any punches.

"I'm not offended one bit, because I feel the same way about them, too. Yours and mine."

She let out a relieved breath, as if she'd really worried that she had said something unforgivable. "Hey, maybe we'll get lucky. Maybe they'll be better grandparents than they were parents. I've heard that can happen."

He held his breath, hearing what she hadn't yet said out loud, grasping the lifeline she'd just thrown him.

She continued. "In the meantime, though, will you understand if I say I'd like for us to give up your house and my apartment, and move to another part of town, away from all of them?"

He didn't answer the question, focused entirely on what it meant. "Does that mean you're going to marry me, Abby?"

She didn't laugh it off or call him silly. Instead she nodded, solemn, sincere. "If you'll still have me."

He bent to brush his mouth against hers. "I'll have

you. I'll have you and take you and want you and love you every day for the rest of my life."

Slipping out from under her, he dropped to the floor of the gazebo, getting on one knee. The first time he'd proposed to her had been over an elegant dinner in a fancy restaurant. He hadn't been on his knees. Now, he wanted her to see just how much he wanted this. Her. *Them*.

"Abigail Bauer, will you do me the honor of becoming my wife?"

She nodded without hesitation, her eyes sparkling with moisture. Tugging the engagement ring off her finger, she dropped it into his hand, then extended her own so he could slide it on all over again.

This time, it felt like more than an engagement. It was a lifelong promise, the first moment of their marriage.

"For richer, for poorer, in sickness and in health," she said.

"In wild, crazy passion and in tenderness, to have and to hold from this day forward," he told her, sealing the deal with a soft kiss.

She tightened her arms around his neck. "You got a deal. Just be warned, I'm going to be insatiable. I think I might be a bit of a nymphomaniac."

"Sounds good to me. I plan to jump your bones every night of the week and twice on Sundays once we're married."

She wagged her eyebrows. "It's Sunday."

Oh, how he liked this new, naughty Abby. "But we're not officially married yet."

Shrugging, she lifted her hand to her coat and slipped the rest of the buttons open. "I think we could make an exception just this once."

The moonlight shining through the slats in the side

of the gazebo danced across her skin—she was luminescent, like one with the night. A mysterious moon goddess meant only for him.

Keith helped her with the final buttons, pushing the coat open, then off, so he could press warm kisses on her bare middle. He moved his mouth to her breasts—kissing her nipple, moistening it until the night air hardened it to a tight, sensitive point of sensation. She shivered, and he covered her with his mouth again, sucking gently, loving the roll of that soft flesh against his tongue.

She twined her fingers in his hair, quivering, sighing. "Do you have any idea how you make me feel? You do realize I was so angry and hurt because I *wanted* you so badly, don't you?"

"I know."

"I want to do this with you forever," she told him, sounding dreamy and tender. "I want us to still do this together when we're old and gray."

He laughed softly. "Even if I have to get my knees replaced, honey, I am so up for that."

She leaned down and caught his mouth in a deep, slow kiss, their tongues tangling in sweet desire. Kissing Abby was one of his favorite things to do on this earth. And now, knowing they were right, and fine, and good, it was even better.

Dying to have her again—slow and hot and sultry this time, rather than fast and frantic—he unfastened his pants. Abby slid forward on the seat, parting her thighs invitingly, the silky dress falling over them. In their frenzy, he'd torn her thong, and she was completely bare beneath the fabric. Bare, soft, wet. He slid his fingertips across her slick sex, glad to see she was every bit as aroused now as he was—even though they'd just had wild sex in the barn.

He hoped it would always be like this. That they'd always desire each other so intensely. And that they never let misunderstandings come between them again.

"Please, Keith," she whispered, leaning closer, until her warm channel brushed against the tip of his cock.

He didn't need any further coaxing. Kissing her again, and twining his hands in her hair, he slid into her slowly, inch by inch, savoring the warmth and the tightness and the sensation that was uniquely Abby.

"I love you so much," she whispered against his mouth.

"I love you, too, Abs."

After just a few strokes, Abby began to take control. While they were still joined, she gently pushed him onto his back, until he lay flat on the floor, then straddled him. Her long hair fell in a brown curtain around them, drops of moonlight sending glimmers of gold dancing through it. He reached up to cup her breast, certain he'd never seen anything more beautiful, more desirable in his life than this woman on top of him.

Though slower this time, it was in no way vanilla sex. Abby took him, rode him, setting the pace and the tone and the depth. She knew what he wanted and he gave her what she needed and together they acknowledged everything that had turned out so right about this very difficult day.

They were right. They were, in fact, just perfect.

BY THE TIME THEY PULLED their clothes into some semblance of order and headed inside, it was very late. The party was still going on full swing, and those who weren't in attendance were probably already asleep, because the inn was silent and still as they entered.

Abby led Keith to her room, unable to keep the smile

off her face. Tiny bubbles of laughter tried to spill from her lips. She couldn't remember any moment when she'd ever been happier—not even the first time Keith had proposed to her, when she'd been younger, starry-eyed, never dreaming that someday sex might be a problem between them.

Now she knew what it was to have an adult relationship, to truly be a woman. To demand what she wanted and make sure her lover knew how much she wanted him, too.

Once inside her room, she locked the door, then dropped her coat and torn dress to the floor. Her shoes, which had been hanging by the straps on one finger, joined them there.

The light was on, and Keith stared at her, as if he'd never seen her before—as if they hadn't just made love by moonlight.

"Three times on Sunday?" she asked, lifting a brow and chuckling.

"Maybe we should write this down so we don't forget by the time we get around to getting married."

Though there was humor in his voice, the words suddenly made her feel both selfish and a little sad. Swallowing, she whispered, "I really don't want it to be too long before we get around to it."

He held her stare. "How soon would you like to do it?"

"Um…tomorrow?"

Keith nodded slowly, not laughing outright as she'd half expected him to. "I'm liking this idea."

"Our families would be upset."

"Even more reason to like it," he said with a boyish grin. "Are you sure you wouldn't mind missing the big, fancy wedding?"

"I just had Amanda's," she said with a shrug. "Honestly, I couldn't imagine anything more wonderful than running away and marrying you right this very minute."

He gave it about ten seconds thought, then leaped to his feet, grabbed her suitcase and started throwing her clothes into it. "Vegas?"

Laughing joyously, she pulled a pair of jeans and a sweater off the bed and shimmied into them. "Absolutely." Then she took his hand and smiled at him, happiness filling her every molecule.

"I love you, Keith. Tomorrow just doesn't seem soon enough to become your wife."

Stepping close, he drew her into his arms. "I love you, too, Abs. We're going to have a great time."

"In Vegas?"

"In our whole marriage."

She nodded, agreeing.

Then, together, they threw the rest of her things in the bag, crept out of the room and down the stairs.

Ten minutes later they were in his rental car, heading back to Chicago. And less than twelve hours after that—one day after she'd broken their engagement, Abby Bauer became Mrs. Keith Manning.

Or, in his words, the goddess of his heart for the rest of his life.

* * * * *

Epilogue

THERE WAS SOMETHING TO BE said for hotel sex.

Reese and Amanda had been lovers for a year, but last night—their wedding night—had been one for the record books.

Funny thing was, it had included no playacting, no props, no naughty games. Just pure heartfelt passion and deep, true love. She knew not every night of their marriage would be as glorious as the first, but oh, had they set the bar pretty damned high.

"Almost ready to go, Mrs. Campbell?" her handsome husband asked, watching her from the other room as she finished putting on her makeup in the bathroom.

"Do we have to?"

"Post-wedding breakfast and we're the main attraction. Sorry, I think we have to."

"Can't we run away like Abby and Keith did?"

Wow, had that been a surprise. Her baby sister had left a note for her at the front desk, saying that she and her fiancée—who had *so* not looked boring in his incredibly sexy costume last night—had eloped.

"I wish we could," Reese said, "considering you're going to have to be the one to break the news to your parents."

She snorted. "Are you kidding? That's one of the few things that could drag me out of this room—getting to see their faces when they find out that Abby is a little more like me than they'd ever thought...or feared!"

Reese understood; he always understood. "I just hope I'm not the one who has to explain if Bonnie forgets to go back to her own room this morning and my mother goes looking for her."

Amanda, who wasn't sure how her husband would feel about his little sister getting lucky with a movie star, turned to stare at him, one brow raised.

"Oh, come on," he said, "you don't *really* think she was going back to her own room, alone, last night, do you?"

"Well, judging by the way they were looking at each other, no, I don't. I just wasn't sure how you'd feel about it."

"I'm not sure yet. Ask me tomorrow, after we find out whether there's more to this than one wild wedding night."

She liked the sound of that. Their wedding, being a wild one, not just for them, but for their friends.

"I guess we weren't the only ones who got lucky."

"Judging by the way Jazz and that guy you work with at the airport were hanging all over each other, I suspect not."

She liked that idea—Jazz and Blake. Stranger things had happened. They said opposites attract. Whether opposites stayed together in the long-term was anyone's guess. But knowing Jazz—and Blake—she suddenly had the feeling they were just what the other needed.

Reese walked into the opulent bathroom and stood behind her, meeting her stare in the window. His hands on her hips, he pulled her back against him, then bent to kiss her neck.

"Last night was amazing," he whispered.

"You mean the part where I beat up some crazy, kidnapping stalker?"

Chuckling, he nibbled her earlobe. "Uh, no, the other part." Wagging his brows he added, "But you being all violent and badass is pretty hot. Maybe we'll have to play tough boxer-chick and hapless trainer."

She giggled, turned in his arms and wrapped her own around his neck. "Are you still going to want to play naughty games with me when we're senior citizens?"

"Absolutely." He kissed her forehead, kissed the tip of her nose, then lightly kissed her lips. "I love you, Mrs. Campbell."

Amanda liked the sound of that—Mrs. Campbell. She knew she was going to like it all the rest of her days.

"Okay, husband, let's go see what craziness everybody else got up to last night."

He smiled down at her. "Or we could stay here awhile longer and get up to a little more craziness ourselves. It is our anniversary, after all."

Hmm. Breakfast, loud family, friends, noise, departures, hugs, complaints, congratulations?

Or hot sex with her brand-new hubby?

What an absolute no-brainer.

"I like the way you think, Reese Campbell, and I can't wait to hear what you have in mind."

He laughed, tugged her tighter, then whispered something extremely naughty in her ear.

"Scratch that. I *really* like the way you think."

Then Amanda and her husband, Reese, proceeded to celebrate the one year anniversary of the day they met... by being just as wild and passionate as they'd been from the very start.

* * * * *

COMING NEXT MONTH

Available October 26, 2010

#573 THE REAL DEAL
Lose Yourself...
Debbi Rawlins

#574 PRIVATE AFFAIRS
Private Scandals
Tori Carrington

#575 NORTHERN ENCOUNTER
Alaskan Heat
Jennifer LaBrecque

#576 TAKING CARE OF BUSINESS
Forbidden Fantasies
Kathy Lyons

#577 ONE WINTER'S NIGHT
Encounters
Lori Borrill

#578 TOUCH AND GO
Michelle Rowen

REQUEST YOUR FREE BOOKS!

2 FREE NOVELS
PLUS 2
FREE GIFTS!

HARLEQUIN®

Blaze™

Red-hot reads!

HARLEQUIN®

A *Romance*

FOR EVERY MOOD™

Spotlight on
Inspirational

Wholesome romances
that touch the heart and soul.

See the next page
to enjoy a sneak peek from
the Love Inspired® Suspense
inspirational series.

*See below for a sneak peek from
our inspirational line, Love Inspired® Suspense*

*Enjoy this heart-stopping excerpt from
RUNNING BLIND
by top author Shirlee McCoy,
available November 2010!*

*The mission trip to Mexico was supposed to be an
adventure. But the thrill turns sour when Jenna Dougherty
and her roommate Magdalena are kidnapped.*

"It's okay. I'm here to help." The voice was as deep as the darkness, but Jenna Dougherty didn't believe the lie. She could do nothing but lie still as hands slid down her arms, felt the rope around her wrists.

"I'm going to use a knife to cut you free, Jenna. Hold still."

The cold blade of a knife pressed close to her head before her gag fell away.

"I—" she started, but her mouth was dry, and she could do nothing but suck in air.

"Shhh. Whatever needs to be said can be said when we're out of here." Nick spoke quietly, his hand gentle on her cheek. There and gone as he sliced through the ropes on her wrists and ankles.

He pulled her upright. "Come on. We may be on borrowed time."

"I can't leave my friend," Jenna rasped out.

"There's no one here. Just us."

"She has to be here." Jenna took a step away.

"There's no one here. Let's go before that changes."

"It's dark. Maybe if we find a light…"

"What did you say?"

"We need to turn on the light. I can't leave until I know that—"

"What can you see, Jenna?"

"Nothing."

"No shadows? No light?"

"No."

"It's broad daylight. There's light spilling in from the window I climbed in through. You can't see it?"

She went cold at his words.

"I can't see anything."

"You've got a nasty bruise on your forehead. Maybe that has something to do with it." His fingers traced the tender flesh on her forehead.

"It doesn't matter *how* it happened. I'm blind!"

Can Nick help Jenna find her friend or will chasing this trail have Jenna running blindly again into danger?

Find out in RUNNING BLIND, available in November 2010 only from Love Inspired Suspense.